W9-AHA-804

RUTHIE'S GIFT

Kimberly Brubaker Bradley

Illustrated by Dave Kramer

A Yearling Book

Published by
Bantam Doubleday Dell Books for Young Readers
a division of
Random House, Inc.
1540 Broadway
New York, New York 10036

If you purchased this book without a cover you should be aware that this book is stolen property. It was reported as "unsold and destroyed" to the publisher and neither the author nor the publisher has received any payment for this "stripped book."

Text copyright © 1998 by Kimberly Brubaker Bradley
Illustrations copyright © 1998 by Dave Kramer

All rights reserved. No part of this book may be reproduced or transmitted in any form or by any means, electronic or mechanical, including photocopying, recording, or by any information storage and retrieval system, without the written permission of the Publisher, except where permitted by law. For information address Delacorte Press, New York, New York 10036.

The trademarks Yearling® and Dell® are registered in the U.S. Patent and Trademark Office and in other countries.

YHBA 4-6 '02-'03

Visit us on the Web! www.randomhouse.com

Educators and librarians, for a variety of teaching tools, visit us at www.randomhouse.com/teachers

ISBN 0-440-41405-9

Reprinted by arrangement with Delacorte Press

Printed in the United States of America

November 1999

10 9 8 7 6 5 4 3

CWO

To my grandmother Ruth Hawk Brubaker,
and in memory of my great-uncle Paul

Contents

1

Too Many Boys

"How many eggs this morning?" Ruthie's mother asked. She walked slow and heavy around the corner of the hot stove and laid a platter of bacon on the table.

"Fifty-seven." Ruthie slid into her chair.

"Not bad," Ruthie's oldest brother, Joe, said approvingly.

"Not bad," Ruthie's favorite brother, Paul, mimicked, dropping his voice low like Joe's.

Joe flushed. He was fifteen, quiet and slow-moving, like the river this time of year. Joe loved the farm and took an interest in every part of it. Paul was nine, just one year older than Ruthie.

He was quick as a spring flood and didn't care for farming at all. Paul was an adventurer.

Ruthie would have liked to be an adventurer, but she was a girl. She grinned at Paul. Of all her brothers, he was the most like her.

Father, Ted, and Luther came in from the barn. Ted whopped Ruthie's head with the back of his hand as he sat down. Ruthie kicked him.

"Ruthie!" Father said.

"He started it!" she protested.

"It was an accident, Ruthie," Ted said mildly. Ruthie knew better than to believe that. Ted was thirteen.

Luther stuck his face near hers. "Are you okay?" he asked solemnly.

"Yes," Ruthie said, making the word sound long and annoyed. Luther was five, and he was always hanging on her.

Mother plucked Charlie off the floor, where he was playing with a wooden horse, and sat him in the high chair. He howled until he noticed the food.

Father said grace. When he finished, instead of saying "Amen" the way he always did, he paused a moment, then added, looking at his hands, "We pray for peace, today and for our future. Amen."

"Amen," Ruthie said. She wondered what that was about. Grown-ups were always talking about war these days, but the war was somewhere far away. There was no need to pray about that war here.

"Amen-pass-the-eggs!" Paul whispered. Ruthie giggled.

"Paul Emory Hawk," Mother warned.

"Sorry." He ducked his head.

Ruthie piled her plate high with bacon, eggs, and toast. She swung her feet beneath her chair, ate, and tried not to worry about school. Today was the first day. She'd heard there were some new families living south of town. Maybe there would be enough new students that school would be different this year. She hoped so. Last year had been horrid.

A glob of egg yolk fell off her fork onto her napkin. "Ruthie!" Mother sounded stern. "Did you muss your blouse?"

Ruthie checked. "No, ma'am."

"Keep yourself clean today, for a change. For this one day you can look like a lady."

"I'll try."

Mother cooked and cleaned, did housework, gardened, and chased after Charlie without ever getting a smudge of dirt on her. Ruthie despaired of being so tidy. She did try. She just couldn't do it. Maybe if she could, school would be easier. The other girls wouldn't scorn her so.

"All of you had better try." Mother's glance swept the table. Joe, Ted, and Paul nodded. Luther nodded too, even though he was too young for school.

Mother leaned back in her chair and ran her hand over her belly. She'd taken to doing that lately.

"Mother," Ruthie said suddenly, "shouldn't I stay home from school? I could watch Charlie for you. And Luther. I could peel potatoes. I could be a big help."

Mother smiled. "Ruthie, you need your education."

"But—" Ruthie made a gesture toward Mother's swollen stomach. In just a few weeks, she was going to have a new baby. A girl, Ruthie hoped fervently. No family could have six boys and only one girl. It would be so unfair to the girl that it would never happen.

"I'll be fine, Ruthie. Aunt Cleone is coming Friday to help out for a while. You go on to school." Ruthie nodded. It was the answer she'd expected.

Mother inspected each of them before they left. She straightened Joe's collar, wiped a smut off Ted's neck, and made Paul tuck his shirttail in. She fussed longest over Ruthie, slicking stray hairs back behind her ears and smoothing and pulling at her new blouse.

"Mother," Ruthie protested. "Mother, I look fine. I look better than the boys."

Mother smiled. "You should. You're my little lady. Now remember that. Remember, you're a lady!" She gave her a kiss and a little swat on the shoulder.

"Remember, you're a lady!" Paul said, once they were on the road.

"Shut up." Ruthie dragged her shiny new boots

through the fine dust in the wheel track. Mother always called her a little lady. Ruthie knew she was no lady. She knew how disappointed Mother must be.

"You're a lady, you're a lady!" Paul taunted.

"Shut up!" Ruthie threw herself at him and knocked him to the ground. Her lunch pail flew open and her apple rolled out. She pounded Paul.

"Ruthie!" Ted pulled her off him. "Look at you!"

Ruthie wiped at a grass stain on her blouse. "I don't care!" she said.

"Paul started it," Joe said mildly. "Don't tease her, Shorty. You know better."

Paul glowered. Ruthie laughed. Paul was barely as tall as she, even though he was older and a boy. He hated being called Shorty.

"Shorty," Ruthie said.

"*Lady.*"

"Enough!" Ted picked up Ruthie's apple and lunch pail and thrust them at her. "Maybe you two babies don't care if you're late for school, but I do."

"Brush your skirt off," Joe told Ruthie. He

took her hand. "Don't worry. You look like a lady to me."

Ruthie scuffed her feet. How could she even hope to be a lady, when she was surrounded by so many boys?

2

The Entire Third Grade

The schoolyard was crowded. Ruthie stood under the mulberry tree beside the schoolhouse and watched her brothers greet the friends they hadn't seen all summer. A trio of girls in gingham—Maude, Alice, and Rosemarie—sauntered past. Maude wrinkled her elfin nose at Ruthie. "There's Ruth Hawk," she whispered in a nasty voice quite loud enough for Ruthie to hear. "I told you she'd be dirty. I don't think she bathes."

Ruthie's fingers curled tight around the handle of her pail. "I'm cleaner than you on the inside, Maude Townsend!" she shouted.

Every pupil in the yard turned and stared.

Maude and Rosemarie burst into giggles, and Alice looked amazed. Ruthie blushed furiously. Father always told her she must keep a clean soul. But she knew that her insides were no cleaner than her outsides. She burned with hatred for sniggering Maude, rude Rosemarie, and even dainty, mincing Alice.

Ruthie couldn't help herself. She threw her lunch pail and schoolbooks to the ground and advanced toward Maude with her fists raised. Maude gave her a scornful look but took a step backward. Ruthie took another step forward. Just as she was about to flatten Maude and rip the ribbons from the girl's braids, someone grabbed her from behind and snatched her clean off the ground.

"Joe!" Ruthie kicked him and squealed. "Put me down! Put me down!"

Joe sat her hard on the firm dirt by the doorstep. "Knock it off!" he growled. "What would Mother say?"

Ruthie felt her eyes fill with tears, but she did not cry. "They're so mean and hateful," she said.

Joe nodded sympathetically. "So hate 'em," he

said. "But don't murder them, Ruthie, not in the schoolyard."

Teacher's bell rang before she could reply. Ruthie got up and smoothed her skirt with dignity. She ignored Joe, Maude, Rosemarie, and Alice too and marched through the door.

Inside the classroom a bevy of new pupils milled around in confusion. Mr. Ames, the teacher, assigned the desks. Ruthie's seatmate was one of the new students, a small black-haired girl named Mary. She smiled shyly at Ruthie.

Ruthie took out her slate. "Are you in third grade, too?" she wrote on it. She passed it to Mary, who looked at it in confusion. Ruthie's heart sank.

"Can you read?" she whispered. Mary shook her head. "Never mind." Ruthie took her slate back.

Her fears were confirmed when Mr. Ames called the third grade forward. She walked alone to the front of the room.

"Ruth Hawk," Mr. Ames said, peering at her over the top of his spectacles, "you're by yourself again. It's an odd coincidence, given that we have over thirty scholars in the school."

"Yes, sir." When Ruthie had been a first-grader there had been three other students in her class, but last year all of them had moved away. She had been the only second-grader. This year there were seven new students, but none was in her grade.

"Perhaps, if you study hard, I could promote you to the fourth grade," Mr. Ames suggested. "You're bright enough, and you could easily keep up with the children in that class. Would you like that?"

Maude, Rosemarie, and Alice were three of the five fourth-graders. The other two were boys. "No, thank you," Ruthie said.

"Very well." He sent her back to her seat.

At home that afternoon Ruthie's mother hugged her tight. "How was it, darling?"

Ruthie smothered a sob against her mother's shoulder. "It happened again. I'm the entire third grade."

Mother's bulky stomach pressed against her ribs. "I'm sorry, dear," Mother said.

"Why do I have to be a lady?" Ruthie wailed. "I hate that Maude Townsend so much. I want to hit her." She didn't tell Mother how close she'd come.

"Ladies don't hate," Mother reproved her gently. "They don't hit, either."

"I know," Ruthie said, "but I want to. She's a very hittable, very hateable person."

"Do your best, Ruthie," was all Mother said.

That was the problem. What if her best wasn't good enough?

Ruthie felt the new baby flutter inside Mother's stomach. She hoped it wasn't wicked to pray for a girl.

3

The Baby Arrives

※

$\mathscr{R}$uthie turned into the farmyard, stopped, and stared. Her lunch pail banged against her shin. Behind her, Joe, Ted, and Paul stopped too. The doctor's black buggy stood beside the barn.

"Where's his horse?" Ruthie asked. Her heart thudded in her chest.

School had been in session for two miserable weeks. It was even worse than last year. At recess the boys wouldn't let her play baseball, because she wasn't good enough, and the girls wouldn't let her play anything. That very day, Maude had refused to let her jump rope with the older girls, even though she let Mary and the other first- and second-grade girls play.

"You're always playing with boys," Maude had accused her, looking down her hateful little nose. "You act just like a boy yourself. You ought to sit on the boys' side of the room. You're not ladylike, and we don't want you around."

Ruthie had pulled Maude's hair, and Mr. Ames had sent her inside and made her write "I will not cause disruptions during noon recess" a hundred times on the chalkboard. She didn't care. She was alone at school, and alone at home.

But now the doctor's buggy had come. Maybe by nightfall her little sister would be here. Maybe then she wouldn't be alone.

"His horse must be inside the barn," Paul guessed. "He's been here a while." His hand tightened around Ruthie's shoulder, but she pushed it away. She walked toward the house slowly.

On the front porch Luther was jumping up and down, bouncing his ball off the side of the house. "The doctor's here!" he yelled when he saw them. "Ruthie, Mother's having the baby!"

"Hush!" Ruthie said. She smiled anxiously at her aunt Dorothy, who came to the door. "Is it here yet?" she asked. She wanted to say, "Is *she* here? My baby sister?" but she didn't dare.

Aunt Dorothy shook her head but smiled back. "Not much longer." She passed a plate of cookies around to them. "You children go off and do your chores now, and then go play. Stay out of the house until I tell you."

Joe grabbed a handful of cookies and headed for the barn. Ted and Paul sat down on the step and stuffed themselves. Ruthie was too anxious to sit or eat.

"Play with me, Ruthie," Luther begged. "Play catch." He pulled at her sleeve. She shook him off.

"Where's Charlie?" she asked.

"Aunt Cleone took him for a walk. If you hurry, you can catch them." Aunt Dorothy smoothed Ruthie's braids. "Don't look so worried. Your mother's good at having babies."

"I know." Ruthie laid her reader on the porch and walked away.

"Play with me!" Luther shouted after her.

"I've got work to do!"

"Ruthie!" Paul called. "Let's play Capture the Flag when chores are done."

Ruthie ignored him too. She did not feel like Capture the Flag. She did not feel like eating cookies. She did not feel like walking, not even with Aunt Cleone, her favorite aunt. She didn't feel like doing her chores, and she didn't want to be near Joe, Ted, babbling Luther, drooling Charlie, or even Paul. None of them understood.

Ruthie sat down in the grass near the cellar door to wait. Her fingers itched with impatience. Finally she crept into the house and retrieved her tatting from her sewing basket in the living room. She heard voices close by and quickly went back outside.

She unfolded her tatting into her hands. It was a small piece of lace, pretty enough for a small baby girl. Ruthie untangled her shuttle and started to work. The boys could do her chores for once. Hang the chickens. She didn't care.

The sun was throwing long shadows across the dying fields by the time Ruthie tied her last knot. She broke the thread with her teeth and smoothed the lace across her knee. It was the nicest, best thing she'd ever made.

"There you are!"

The voice made Ruthie jump. She shoved the lace into her apron pocket and turned.

Aunt Cleone smiled down at her. "Come into the house," she offered.

"The baby?" Ruthie asked.

"Beautiful, perfect, and healthy," Aunt Cleone said. "He's a fine little boy."

4

Ruthie Leaves

❦

*R*uthie tore away from Aunt Cleone's hand. She ran around the house, trampled her mother's flower bed, and dashed into the privy. She slammed the wooden latch shut, sat down on the seat, and bawled.

A boy. A boy. The baby she had hoped and prayed for was a *boy*. Another brother. She was surrounded. Ruthie huddled her head in her arms and sobbed.

She was alone everywhere. The new baby was a boy. She had six brothers now.

"Ruthie, dear!" Aunt Cleone rapped on the privy door. "Come out, please. I know you're disappointed, sweetheart, but he is a beautiful little baby, and your mother wants to see you."

Ruthie plugged her ears and didn't budge.

A fierce pounding replaced Aunt Cleone's gentle taps. "Ruthie!" shouted Ted. "If you don't come out now, I'm turning this over on your head!"

Ruthie jumped up and threw open the door. She butted her head into Ted's belly and sent him sprawling. She ran past the house and out of the yard. She ran down the road. She ran away.

No one followed. Soon Ruthie quit running and quit crying. She noticed the yellow sunlight filtering through the autumn leaves. She climbed down the riverbank and washed her face in the cold, slow-moving water. She took off her boots and stockings. She kept walking. She wasn't going back, not to that house full of boys.

At the Sutters' drive she stopped. They called it the Sutters' drive because the Sutter family had once lived at the end of it, but they had moved away long ago. Ruthie and her brothers were forbidden to play in the empty farmhouse or barns.

But now Ruthie could hear voices at the end of the drive. Girls' voices, laughing. Girls. She walked toward them.

A big freight wagon stood in front of the house, and men were unloading furniture and boxes from it. Two little girls were climbing on the tailgate. Their hair was braided, like Ruthie's, and their feet were bare. Most amazing of all—they looked exactly alike!

"Hello!" one of them said when she saw Ruthie. "Are you a neighbor?"

"I guess so." Ruthie looked from one to the other. She felt like she was seeing double.

"I'm Hallie," said the first little girl.

"I'm Mallie," said the other.

"We're twins," Hallie added.

Ruthie had heard of twins, but she had never seen any before. "How do I tell you apart?" she asked.

The twins laughed. "That's easy," explained Mallie. "Hallie's got a chipped front tooth."

Hallie opened her mouth wide and showed it to Ruthie. "I did it this spring. Before that, no one could tell who we were. Mother used to

make us wear different-colored ribbons so the teacher could tell us apart at school."

"At recess we used to switch," Hallie added with a wicked grin that was not ladylike at all.

"What grade are you in?" Ruthie asked.

"Third," they said together.

Ruthie's heart swelled. She took a very deep breath. "I'm Ruth Hawk," she said. "We live on the next farm. If you walk down the road tomorrow, I'll show you the way to school. You . . . you're going to be in my class. There'll be three of us now." She felt so relieved she nearly cried. Three sounded so much friendlier than one. And all three of them girls.

Hallie jumped out of the wagon bed, raising a cloud of dust. Mallie followed. "Good," Hallie said. "We've been to school two weeks already, can you believe that? In Harlan, where we lived before. Mother made us go even though she knew we were moving here."

"She wanted us out of the house," said Mallie. "She's busy with the new baby."

"We have a new baby, too," Ruthie said. "He was born today."

"Ours is two months old, and tiresome!" said Mallie. "She doesn't ever smile, and she cries all the time. Her name is Sarah. She spits up."

"I don't think our baby has a name yet," Ruthie said. Maybe he did. Ruthie felt sorry that she hadn't asked. "It's all boys at my house," she said to Hallie and Mallie. "Six of them. I'm in the middle, and I hate it."

Hallie slipped her arm around Ruthie's waist. "There are no boys here," she said fiercely.

"Come on," added Mallie. "We'll show you our sheep."

Before Ruthie could see the sheep, Hallie and Mallie's mother called them to the house. "I need you to help me unpack now," she told them. "You can play tomorrow or the next day. Is this a new friend?" She smiled at Ruthie in a friendly fashion.

"Mother, this is Ruth Hawk," Hallie said politely. "She's our neighbor, and she's going to take us to school tomorrow." Clearly Hallie could act like a lady sometimes.

"Pleased to meet you, Ruthie," Hallie and Mallie's mother said. "I'm Mrs. Graber."

"Pleased to meet you, Mrs. Graber," Ruthie recited. She could act like a lady sometimes, too. "I know my mother will come visit," she added, "only probably not for a few days. She had a baby this afternoon."

"Goodness," Mrs. Graber said. "Then perhaps I should visit her."

"It was a boy," Ruthie said, with a sudden burst of anger. "Another boy. We've got nothing but boys, and I hate them!"

Mrs. Graber's face became sad. Mallie pulled on Ruthie's hand. "Come look at our baby," she ordered. In the corner of the kitchen, a tiny baby, wrapped in a white blanket, lay sleeping in an empty egg box. Her little fists were curled tightly around her face, and one small lock of dark hair peeked out from her bonnet. Ruthie could not remember when Luther or Charlie had been so small.

"It's a beautiful baby." She reached out with one finger to touch the baby's hand. "Is it really a girl?"

"Her name is Sarah," Mrs. Graber said.

"We had a boy," Hallie said. "His name was Samuel. He died."

"We miss him," Mallie added.

Ruthie looked up in horror. "Oh," she said. "Oh, I don't think my baby is going to die."

"Of course not," Mrs. Graber said gently, putting her arm around Ruthie's shoulders. "He'll be a fine baby, just like Sarah. And it must be very hard for you not to have any sisters. You should come here often to play with Hallie and Mallie."

"I will," Ruthie said. She found that she was crying again. "Only now I have to go home, right away." She shook herself free from the Grabers and ran out of the house.

"We'll see you tomorrow!" Mallie called after her.

5

Happy Birthday, Boiled Bert

❦

*R*uthie ran all the way home. In the farmyard, the doctor's buggy was gone. Ruthie's father was standing on the front porch, lighting his pipe.

"Well, daughter," he said gravely. "You're covered in dust. And where are your shoes?"

Ruthie didn't know. "Can I see Mother?" she asked.

Her father tapped her on the head and nodded. "Go quietly, now. She's tired."

Ruthie knocked gently on her mother's door and slid into the room. "Mama?"

"Hello, Ruthie." Her mother was lying in bed,

surrounded by pillows. She looked worn out but happy. "I wondered where you were," she said.

"I went to the Sutters' place." Ruthie sat down on the edge of the bed. Her mother reached for her hand and held it. "New people are moving in," Ruthie said. "Their name is Graber. Mr. Graber had a dry-goods store in Harlan, but he gave it up because he's better at farming." Hallie and Mallie had told Ruthie that. "Mrs. Graber says she'll come visiting soon. Mama, where's the baby?"

"Right here." Ruthie's mother nudged a soft pillow-shape next to her, and Ruthie saw that it was indeed a sleeping baby, wrapped in a blanket.

Ruthie stood. She carefully pushed the blanket away from her new brother's face. "He looks like a boiled beet," she said. "And his ears are just like baby mouse ears."

"He'll turn out fine," Mother said. "Your face was that red once, too, and your ears were small and folded. He'll be a pretty baby. All of you children were pretty babies."

"He's a pretty baby now," Ruthie said

staunchly. "He's much prettier than the Grabers' baby. What's his name?"

"Bert," said Mother. "Bert St. Clair Hawk."

Ruthie giggled. "Boiled-Beet Bert." Then she remembered the piece of lace. She drew it out of her apron pocket. "I made this," she said, handing it to her mother. "For the baby. Before I knew he was a boy."

Mother fanned it out between her fingers. "Why, Ruthie, this is lovely," she said. "You did a very nice job."

"But boys don't wear lace," Ruthie said miserably. "And I made it just for him."

Mrs. Hawk smiled. "Boys wear lace sometimes," she said. "I'm going to make Bert a new bonnet to wear to his christening, and your lace will be the very thing to trim it. Thank you." She put the lace on the bedside table. "I know you wanted a girl."

"You couldn't help having a boy," Ruthie said. "I just thought maybe God would give you a girl this time."

Mother pushed the hair back from Ruthie's face. "God gave me you."

"I'm the only girl."

"You're a good girl, and I love you."

"But I'm not a lady." Ruthie couldn't explain how sorry she was. "I'm just not."

"You will be." Suddenly Mother looked very tired.

Ruthie kissed her. "Shall I bring you some supper?" she asked.

Her mother smiled and said yes. "Ruthie," she added as Ruthie was going out the door, "are there any little girls in the new family next door?"

"Two, plus a baby." Ruthie gave a skip. "Two my age, and they look just alike, and they're going to school with me tomorrow. And Hallie has a chipped tooth, so I don't think she can be entirely ladylike, do you?"

"Probably not," Mother replied.

"So," said Ruthie, "I think we shall be friends." She waved at the pillow-shape. "Happy birthday, Boiled Bert," she said, and ran down the hall. She could smell Aunt Cleone's cooking.

6

A For-Real Invitation

⚜

*B*oiled Bert wailed and smelled and was not much use, but school improved immediately. Hallie and Mallie shared the seat across the aisle from Ruthie. All three shared a jump rope during recess, and sometimes they played together on Saturdays. Kind Mrs. Graber came for tea and became Mother's good friend.

In late October Ruthie ran home from school with her cheeks flushed from excitement. "Look, Mother!" she said. She spread a crumpled piece of paper on the kitchen table. "It's a for-real invitation," she said. "To Hallie and Mallie's. To spend the night. We're going to make caramels

Dear Ruthie,
You are invited to
spend the night at
our house this Friday
Love,
Hallie and Mallie

and tea. We're going to scramble eggs for our supper. Oh, Mother, may I go? Please?"

Mother was nursing Bert. She read the invitation and smiled. "You'll have a lovely time," she said. "Of course you may go. Only mind your manners."

"I'll be a perfect lady," Ruthie promised. She would, no matter what. "I'll make you proud." It would be easy to be a lady at Hallie and Mallie's house, where there weren't any boys.

"Tomorrow, it's tomorrow," she said. "I can't

wait." She jumped up from the table and took an apple out of the cupboard. "No boys!" She spun around the floor. "No boys!"

"What's got into you?" Paul asked, coming into the room.

"Nothing," Ruthie said. "It's my private business."

"Nuts to you," Paul retorted, but he grinned. "Ma, my pants are too short. Look. I'm growing." He held his leg up for them to see.

Mother smiled at him. "I'll drop the hem tonight," she promised.

"And my Sunday pair?"

"By Sunday," she said.

"Turn around," he said to Ruthie. He stood back-to-back against her. "Who's taller?"

Ruthie stood on her toes. Paul laughed and stood on his.

"I believe you're a whole inch bigger," Mother told him. Paul strutted like a cockerel.

"It wouldn't be ladylike to be tall," Ruthie replied. She bragged, "I'm going to the Grabers' to spend the night tomorrow. We're going to make caramels."

"Invite them to stay here," Paul said. "I like that Hallie."

Mother laughed. "How can you tell them apart, Paul? I can't, unless they're smiling."

Paul grinned. "Hallie runs faster." Hallie was louder, too. Sometimes she got in trouble for talking at school.

Ruthie was entranced by Paul's suggestion. "Oh, could I?" she asked. "Could they come here—next week, after I go there? Please?"

"Where would they sleep?" Paul asked. "You couldn't stick them in the closet."

Mother and Father slept in the downstairs bedroom, and baby Bert slept with them in his cradle. There were two upstairs bedrooms. One was supposed to be Ruthie's alone, but Luther still slept there on the trundle bed, and now that Bert had the cradle, Charlie had crowded in with Luther, and Aunt Cleone was sleeping on the daybed beside the window. She would be staying with them another month, until Bert was bigger and Mother wasn't so tired.

"If it weren't for all you stupid boys, I could have my own room," she said.

Mother gave her a warning look. "You're lucky enough to have a roof over your head."

Ruthie knew better than to argue that. "We could stay in the hayloft," she suggested.

"Not this late in the year," Mother objected. "But as you are accepting their invitation, by rights you should invite them here, too. The little boys can stay with the big boys for one night. Perhaps Cleone will sleep on the davenport if you ask her nicely."

Ruthie was in transports. After chores and supper, but before she started her homework, she carefully wrote out two invitations of her own, to give to Hallie and Mallie the next day. Mother added a note for their mother. Ruthie tucked them inside a schoolbook and felt at peace with the world.

7

The House with No Boys

~~~

The next day Ruthie walked home from school arm in arm with the Graber twins. "I'll help you do your chores first," Ruthie said. "Then we can play."

Hallie giggled. "We don't have chores until after supper," she said. "We have to wash and dry the dishes, but that's all."

Ruthie was amazed. "Who does the chickens?" she asked. "Who waters the garden?"

Mallie shrugged. "Mother, when we're at school. The first thing we do is eat cookies."

"We don't have as many chickens as you," Hallie added. "We've only got a couple dozen."

"I know what," said Mallie. "After we eat our cookies, let's dress the cats."

Hallie and Mallie had three kittens that were completely tame. They lived under the front porch. Hallie scooped them out and handed one each to her sister and Ruthie. "We call them Wynken, Blynken, and Nod," she said to Ruthie. "You've got Blynken." She led the way into the kitchen.

"You take them in the house?" Ruthie asked, amazed again.

"Sure," Mallie said. She called a hello to her mother.

"My mother won't allow it," Ruthie said. "She says we've got enough animals inside already."

Hallie and Mallie looked blank.

"My brothers," Ruthie explained. The twins laughed.

Mrs. Graber gave them each a cookie and a glass of fresh milk. Hallie went upstairs and brought down an armful of tiny doll clothes. "Let's see what fits," she said. She grabbed Nod, who was on the table inspecting the empty milk glasses, and pulled a patterned dress over his head. She pushed his paws through the sleeves and buttoned the bodice across his back. Nod purred.

"I'll take the gray flannel for Wynken," Mallie said. "It goes so well with his striped fur."

Ruthie tied a bonnet on Blynken. She picked up a pair of drawers.

"He can't wear those," Mallie said. "There's no hole for his tail."

"We could cut one," Hallie suggested. Mallie pursed her lips. "Maybe not," Hallie said. To Ruthie she added, "Mallie just made those last week."

"Did you make all these clothes?" Ruthie asked. Some of them were exquisite, with hem-stitching and gathered lace.

"Mother made the best ones, but we made most of them. Our grandma lets us have her sewing scraps." Mallie carefully settled a cap over Wynken's ears. She rubbed his belly.

Soon they had the cats as dressed as cats could be. Mallie borrowed baby Sarah's carriage, and they put the cats inside and strolled them up and down the lane. The cats sat up and watched the scenery. They seemed to be enjoying themselves.

"Do you take Sarah for walks?" Ruthie asked.

"Not yet," Hallie said. "Mother says she's too young."

"Soon," said Mallie. "Soon we'll help dress her and change her and everything. When she's just a little bigger, Mother says."

Ruthie had already dressed Bert twice. She didn't say so; it might sound like bragging. She sniffed the autumn air and smiled.

Suddenly the cats had had enough. They leaped out of the carriage and ran. Hallie, Mallie, and Ruthie ran after them. The cats ran through the door of the barn and scampered up the ladder to the loft. The girls looked up. Three cats in dresses and bonnets looked down. The girls laughed.

"Let's get them." Ruthie started up the ladder. Hallie and Mallie followed. Wynken, Blynken, and Nod ran across the loft. They disappeared behind the enormous stack of hay bales that filled most of the space.

"That's that," Hallie said.

Ruthie looked around. The Grabers' barn looked just like their big barn at home. On the main floor, the doors opened wide enough for a wagon to be pulled right inside. Stalls lined the walls. The roof peaked high above the loft floor, and a rope hung from one of the center beams. It dangled between the sides of the loft, far above the main floor.

"I dare you to swing on that rope," Ruthie said to Mallie.

Mallie looked shocked. "I'd be killed!"

Ruthie shrugged. "We have a rope. My brothers swing on it all the time." This was not quite true. Ted swung on it sometimes, and Paul had once, on Ruthie's dare.

"I bet you haven't," Hallie declared.

"I would," Ruthie said.

"Okay. Do it. I dare you."

Ruthie took a deep breath. She backed up against the hay, ran as hard as she could, and jumped into the open air, reaching for the rope. She felt it hit her hands. She grabbed it. "Wheeee," she shouted, to show the twins she wasn't afraid.

The rough rope slid through her hands. Ruthie tried to hang on, but she slid right off the end. She fell ten feet to the main floor and landed flat on her back. The air left her lungs in one hard burst, and she couldn't breathe. The walls swayed dizzily around her.

"Ruthie!" Hallie and Mallie scrambled down the ladder. "Ruthie," Mallie cried anxiously, "Ruthie, are you dead?"

Hallie ran for her father. By the time Mr. Graber arrived, Ruthie could breathe again. She felt weak and unsteady. Mr. Graber prodded her back and limbs before he would allow her to move. Finally he pulled her up. He looked at the three girls.

"I fell out of the loft," Ruthie said.

Mr. Graber examined the raw red marks on Ruthie's palms. He looked at the rope swinging above them. "I see," he said. "Should I be taking you home?"

"Oh, no," Ruthie said shakily. "I'm fine now. I promise." Her head ached and her stomach felt sick, but not for anything would she go home.

Mrs. Graber put goose grease on Ruthie's hands, but they still hurt so much she could barely use them. She couldn't help Hallie and Mallie scramble eggs or make caramels or tea, and she couldn't hold Sarah. However, she could eat the eggs and caramels, and drink the hot sweet tea.

Before supper, Mr. Graber prayed for peace, the way Ruthie's father did every night now. For some reason this comforted Ruthie. After supper they sat around the coal stove in the parlor, listened to Mrs. Graber tell stories, and dressed the cats for bed, and that night Ruthie slept between Hallie and Mallie in their high, soft bed under a white quilted coverlet. She had never felt so happy.

"I can't believe you took that dare," Hallie said, her voice full of drowsy admiration. "You'd do about anything, wouldn't you?"

Ruthie leaned back into her feather pillow. She ignored her smarting hands and the nagging thought that ladies didn't take dares. She felt brave and strong. "I reckon I would," she said with pride.

8

In the Graveyard

The next Friday Hallie and Mallie came home with Ruthie. Ruthie led them up to her bedroom and showed them where they could lay their things. Mother had moved the trundle bed to the boys' room, and Aunt Cleone had gone into town to stay with Ruthie's grandmother for the night.

Hallie and Mallie admired the old-fashioned quilt on Ruthie's bed. They looked out her window at the orchard, and Ruthie pointed out the long rows of strawberries, covered in straw against the cold, in the flatland near the river.

"I have to do my chores before we can play," she said. Hallie and Mallie offered to help.

Even the chickens seemed to realize that it was a special day, because they pecked her less than usual. Ruthie found a few eggs that she'd missed in the morning, and carefully set them in the egg crate.

The boys were cleaning out the barn and giving the animals their evening feed. Paul kept coming out to the henhouse to see how they were doing.

"Go away," Ruthie told him crossly after the third time. She didn't want to share her friends.

Paul just grinned. He tipped his hat toward Hallie and sauntered back to the barn. A few minutes later he was out again. "Want to play Capture the Flag?" he asked.

"No!" Ruthie said. "We're going down to the river." She had started to build a playhouse there. Hallie and Mallie had not seen it yet.

"What's Capture the Flag?" Hallie asked, looking interested.

"Oh! It's fun. I'll see if Ted and Joe want to play." Paul disappeared.

"We want to go down to the river," Ruthie told Hallie.

Hallie shrugged. "Can't we do this first?" she asked.

Mallie nodded, looking eager. "We never have enough people at home for games."

Company had to have their own way. "I guess so," Ruthie said reluctantly. "As long as we don't play too long."

Ted was eager to play, and so was Joe. Luther ran about with his face flushed with joy. He hung on Hallie and Mallie's hands, and they let him, and they even laughed and tried to swing him. Ruthie was disgusted. They all trooped out to the meadow behind the orchard, where the cows grazed in summer. Hallie and Mallie had never played Capture the Flag. Paul explained the rules to them while Ruthie simmered. The sun was already beginning to set. She wanted to go down to the river.

After Capture the Flag Ted suggested they play Kick the Can. "I'll take Hallie on my team," Paul said quickly.

"I'll take Mallie on mine," Ted responded.

"No!" Ruthie said. "We're not playing with you boys anymore. We're not!" She stomped her foot.

"But Ruthie," Mallie protested, "we're having fun."

"I'm not!" Ruthie said. "I don't want to play anymore."

Joe caught Ruthie by the arm. "They're company," he whispered. "Mind your manners. They're your friends."

"I'll just sit here while you play," Ruthie said, folding her arms around her knees. "When you're done we'll go see my playhouse."

To her surprise, the twins let her sit while everyone else played Kick the Can. Ted's team won three times in a row, because he could run faster than anyone.

"Let's go play in the graveyard," Paul suggested.

"No!" said Ruthie.

"What graveyard?" asked Hallie.

"Come on, we'll show you!" The boys ran ahead, Luther tugging at Mallie's hand. The twins followed the boys, and Ruthie walked slowly and ungraciously after them.

The graveyard adjoined the orchard on the side closest to the house. It was so old that the lettering on the stones had been worn smooth, and you could no longer tell who was buried there. A sagging iron fence surrounded the plot.

Ruthie stood by the gate. "We're not allowed to play in there!" she shouted. "Paul! Ted! Mother said!"

Even Joe laughed at her. "Ruthie, you come in here all the time," he said. "You can't tell on us, or we'll tell on you."

"Look, Hallie," Paul said, climbing on one of the stones. "This one's loose." He sat on top of it and rocked his weight back and forth. The stone lurched sideways, one edge coming all the way out of the ground.

"Let's play Graveyard Tag," Ted suggested. Paul rocked his gravestone harder.

Ruthie grabbed one of the apples that had fallen near the fence. She hurled it at Paul's head. Paul ducked. The apple hit Mallie's cheek.

Mallie burst into tears.

"I'm sorry!" Ruthie started to run toward her friend.

Paul lost his balance and fell over sideways. He put his hand to the ground to catch himself. The

heavy gravestone rocked down and crushed it. Paul screamed.

For a second no one knew what to do. They surrounded Paul, who lay on the ground in agony. Joe and Ted rocked the stone off his mangled hand, and Ruthie helped pull it free. She could barely stand to look at it. Joe ran for the house.

"He's bleeding," Hallie gasped.

Ruthie searched her pockets for the handkerchief Mother made her carry. She wrapped it around Paul's hand, but the blood soaked through immediately. "Ted, take off your shirt," Ruthie ordered. She used it as another bandage. Paul had turned ghastly white and was shivering, as if he were suddenly freezing cold. "Stand up," Ruthie said. "We've got to get home."

"I can't stand up," Paul said.

"Yes, you can." Ruthie pulled on his good arm. She had blood all over her dress. The only thing she could think of was getting Paul home.

They started walking through the orchard. Luther ran ahead, shouting for Mother. Ted and Ruthie supported Paul.

Before they were halfway there Father and Mother came running. Father picked Paul up and rushed him back to the house. Ruthie could see Joe hitching Mother's mare to the surrey. He would go for the doctor as fast as he could.

Ruthie slowed. She was breathing heavily and her heart pounded. She turned to look at her friends. Hallie and Mallie were holding hands, and they were both crying. Mallie had a smear of rotten apple flesh running down the side of her face.

Ruthie reached out to wipe it off. She was surprised to see that her fingers were covered with Paul's blood.

Mallie shrank away. "You really *aren't* a lady, are you, Ruth Hawk?" she asked.

Hallie drew her sister closer. "We're going home," she said. "We're not staying here anymore."

9

Poor Paul

Ruthie was in utter misery. Mother had wrapped Paul's hand tightly to control the bleeding, and Father had given him a slug of brandy. They had carried him upstairs, but everyone in the house could still hear him sobbing. Ruthie tried to do her schoolwork in the kitchen, but after a while she couldn't stand listening to Paul any longer. She went to the barn and hid in the hayloft.

The doctor came within two hours. Ruthie hung over the edge of the loft and watched Joe care for the doctor's horse and for Mother's mare.

"That you, Ruthie?" Joe asked without looking up.

"Oh, Joe!" She scrambled down the ladder and clung to him for a moment.

"Here," he said gently, handing her a bucket. She nodded and went to the pump.

"I didn't mean to do it," she said. "I never meant for that to happen."

Joe turned to her, looking puzzled and serious. "Why—"

"I threw that apple and it hit Mallie and it made Paul fall!"

He went to her and shook her gently by the shoulders. "Of course you didn't mean it. It wasn't your fault Paul was hurt. You said we weren't supposed to play in the graveyard. You were right. We were all to blame."

"Hallie and Mallie hate me now. Probably so does Paul. I was aiming for Paul. I was so mad at him."

Joe sat down in the loose hay. Ruthie slumped next to him. "Mallie said I wasn't a lady," Ruthie continued. "And it's true."

"You weren't a lady before, and she liked you fine," Joe pointed out. "They'll get over it. Probably the gore just spooked them some. I know it did me."

"Paul's going to hate me. He doesn't like me much these days anyway. Last year he played catch with me at recess."

"You play with Hallie and Mallie now. He plays with his friends. Plus, he's trying to grow up. He wants to be like Ted."

Ruthie snorted. "Ted wants to be like you."

"And I want to be like them," Joe said quietly. "We can't ever get exactly what we want. Paul won't blame you, Ruthie. He's not the sort. He knows it was an accident."

"You do so get what you want," Ruthie said bitterly. It was true. The boys were allowed to ride horses, swim in the river, and wear pants and climb trees, and she wasn't. All because she was a girl.

"I'd like to stay on the farm forever, and I can't," Joe said. "I'd like to be Paul's age, out of danger."

Ruthie didn't understand the sadness in his voice. She didn't know what he meant and she didn't much care.

The doctor had come out of the house. Ruthie rushed up to him. "Is he okay?" she asked. "Will he die?" She knew of a farmer across town who had mangled his foot in a hay mower. He had died from infection a week later.

The doctor patted her cheek. "I don't believe so," he said. "He lost part of a finger, but the rest of his hand was spared. He should have the use of it still."

No sooner had the doctor left than they heard the sound of another horse. It was Mr. Graber, riding up the lane. Mother came to the door. "How's your boy?" he asked, dismounting. Ruthie hung about to hear the answer.

Mother's face was drawn and anxious. "He's had some morphine. He's sleeping now."

Mr. Graber looked sorry. "Amelia says she'll bring a pudding by tomorrow," he said. "The girls were some shaken up." Mother looked confused.

"Hallie and Mallie were here," Ruthie reminded her. "They were going to spend the night."

"That's right. I'd forgotten." Mother talked softly to Mr. Graber for a moment. Ruthie remembered Hallie and Mallie's overnight things. She fetched them from the bedroom and gave them to Mr. Graber. He thanked her and went home. Ruthie followed Mother into the house.

In the kitchen, Luther was crying. "Comfort him, Ruthie," Mother ordered. Ruthie sat and drew Luther onto her lap.

"You're getting too big," she told him. She wished she were young enough to sit on someone's lap.

"Poor Paul," Luther sobbed. "Poor Paul." His tears and snot wet her collar. Ruthie gritted her teeth. She watched Mother draw a washtub full of cold water and set Paul's bloody clothes to soak. "Let me have your apron and sweater," she told Ruthie. Ruthie took them off, and Mother added them to the tub.

"I've got blood on my stockings too," Ruthie whispered. "And my dress."

"Take them off," Mother said. Ruthie stripped to her petticoats and long winter underwear. "Paul will be okay," Mother added.

"I was so scared!"

Mother put her arms around Ruthie. "You were my brave girl. Ted said you thought fast and acted faster."

"Everyone else just stood there," Ruthie said. "It was awful." She buried her face in her mother's shoulder.

"You did well," Mother said.

"Mallie said I wasn't a lady," Ruthie said.

"You certainly were a lady," Mother said firmly. "You handled yourself well in a crisis, just as every lady should. You're a farmer's daughter; you'll never have fancy dresses or an elegant life. That's not what makes a lady. A lady is how you behave."

Ruthie couldn't bear to tell Mother the truth. She hadn't behaved well. She'd lost her temper and thrown that apple. She wasn't a lady at all. She wasn't a good sister or a good friend. She wasn't a boy. "I'm not anything," she whispered. Only Luther heard.

10

How a Lady Should Act

❧

*P*aul's finger stump and the rest of his hand healed cleanly. He missed school for two weeks. He couldn't go outside, because he couldn't risk getting his bandage soiled, and he grew fractious and bored. Mother said it was his own fault. She said she hoped everyone would stay out of the graveyard from now on.

Ruthie avoided Paul as much as she could. She couldn't stand the sight of his injury. "Hey, Ruthie," he pleaded when she came home from school, "what happened today? Tell me about it."

"Nothing," she said, grabbing her egg basket as she shot out the door. Luther tailed her, as usual.

"Paul's mad," he reported. "He yelled at Charlie and me today. Charlie cried."

"So?" Ruthie didn't look at Luther either. She didn't want to feel responsible. Usually Paul was kind to the babies, far kinder than she was.

"So I wish I could go to school with you. Can I help look for eggs?"

"No," Ruthie said. "It's a girl's job."

Hallie and Mallie were cool toward her now. They still walked to school with her and her brothers, because they had no choice, but they jumped rope at recess with Maude, Rosemarie, and Alice. Ruthie thought her heart would break. She didn't know how to tell them how sorry she was.

"Maude's got a Kewpie doll," Hallie reported one morning, the first day Paul went back to school.

"I know." Ruthie had seen it. She wanted it so badly she would steal for it, but she never got the chance. Maude carried it in her skirt pocket.

"We might get Kewpie dolls for Christmas," Hallie said.

Ruthie scratched at her neck. Her winter underwear itched. She didn't say anything. She knew she wouldn't get a doll for Christmas. She had one already, a battered rag doll left over from when she was a baby. She preferred to play with Bert, who had at last learned to smile.

"We will not," Mallie said to her sister. "Quit trying to be mean. We won't get any dolls for Christmas, and you know it." Hallie scowled. "The new farm cost a lot of money," Mallie continued. "There's none left until the lambs come in the spring."

Ruthie nodded. "It's a bad year," she said. Father had said so. "We always get stockings and underwear for Christmas. We have to, there are so many of us."

Mallie's face took on a pinched, angry look, and Hallie went silent. Ruthie wondered what she could have said wrong. Hallie looked up the road at Ruthie's brothers, who were far ahead of them. Suddenly she sat down on the grass. "Look at this," she said, unbuttoning her boot and pulling it off. "I wish *we* would get new stockings for Christmas."

Ruthie looked at Hallie's long black stocking. At the end near the foot it didn't look like a stocking at all. It didn't have a heel or proper toe; it was just a tube of knitted yarn, sewn shut.

"My cousins sent us a box of old clothes," Hallie said. Her eyes brimmed with tears. "The stockings had horrible holes in them, so Mother cut the feet off and sewed the legs shut again."

"They don't fit right," Mallie added. "They bunch around our ankles."

"But we haven't got money for more, so we have to wear them." Hallie's voice was bitter.

"But no one can see them," Ruthie said.

"That's one comfort." Hallie put her boot back on. She struggled to button it without a buttonhook. Ruthie and Mallie helped her, but it took a long time.

They ran to the schoolhouse. All of the other children were inside. Mr. Ames marked them tardy. Ruthie ignored her brothers' looks and silently took out her speller.

"Ruthie was tardy today," Paul announced the instant he was home.

Mother turned from the stove. "Oh, Ruthie! Why?"

Ruthie couldn't explain about the stockings. If Paul heard, he might tease Hallie and Mallie at school. They would be humiliated. "We were playing," she said. She glared at Paul. If he hadn't still been hurt, she would have kicked him. She never tattled on him. Even if he did hate her, it was a mean trick to tattle.

"You know better," Mother scolded.

"I know." Ruthie put her books on the table. She picked Bert up from his basket and smelled his soft baby hair. Charlie came up to her and whined to be held. She sat down on the bench and pulled Charlie up beside her. Bert grabbed at her braid. Charlie laughed.

"It's not how a lady should act," Mother continued.

"I have no interest in being a lady," Ruthie said.

"And yet you will be one," Mother said.

"Why?" Ruthie shouted. Charlie looked startled, and Bert began to cry. She soothed him against her shoulder and lowered her voice.

"Why do I have to? You're always picking on me! You don't pick on the boys!"

Mother gave Paul a look and he shot out of the room, dragging Charlie with him. Mother sat down and took Bert from Ruthie. "No one is picking on you," she said at last, in a tone that brooked no argument. "You are a girl. Girls grow up to become women, and women must always be ladies. You get into scrapes worse than your brothers, Ruthie. You are going to have to be firm with yourself. But I believe you can do it, and you will do it, because I say so."

Ruthie lowered her eyes. "Yes, ma'am." She took a deep breath. "It would be easier to be a lady if I had a sister."

"Perhaps someday you might have one."

"Can I pretend Bert is a girl? I could call him Bertha."

Mother's lips twitched. "No. You may not."

Ruthie sighed. "Hallie and Mallie hardly even talk to me. They went over to Alice's house last weekend." It had been Alice's birthday. There had been a party with cake, and Ruthie was not invited.

Mother brushed Ruthie's hair from her forehead. "I know. I'm sorry, dear. I'm surprised Paul's accident affected them so."

"They were a little upset with me already."

"I see." Mother didn't ask questions. "Get your chores done now. Keep trying. You'll be a lady yet."

11

Clarinda

*J*ust before Thanksgiving Father brought home the new Sears Roebuck catalog. The whole family spent the evening admiring the wonderful goods it advertised for sale. Father picked out a new piece of harness he needed for the team. Mother ordered a covered casserole and a butter dish to replace one Charlie had broken. She looked longingly at the Hoosier cabinets, then shook her head and pushed the catalog aside. "Perhaps next year, when things are better," Father said, and Mother nodded.

The boys and Ruthie spent ages admiring the toys. They clustered around the catalog at the table. Ted slowly turned the pages. "Ugh, dolls," he said, and flipped forward to the electric trains.

"Give that back!" Ruthie grabbed the catalog. "I want to see."

"C'mon, Ruthie, you don't want a doll," Ted grumbled. "You've already got one."

Ruthie's rag doll was named Dottie. Paul had thrown her into the pigpen years ago, on a dare from Ted, and Luther had spit up on her when he was a baby. Dottie was not very nice anymore.

Ted tried to take the catalog from Ruthie. She turned so that her shoulder blocked him.

" 'Guaranteed Unbreakable,' " Paul read, over her other shoulder. "That's the kind of doll you need, all right."

"With you stupid boys always messing with my stuff," Ruthie retorted. "Poor Dottie." The unbreakable dolls were lovely, but they were very expensive. Some of them cost as much as two dollars.

"Let us see," Paul said. "You can have the book yourself later, if you have to look at dolls."

"No," said Ruthie.

"Boys," Mother cautioned, "let your sister have a turn."

"We will," said Ted. "Later."

"No!" Ruthie picked up the catalog and moved to the far end of the table.

She turned the page. Her mouth dropped open. There, in the upper corner, was the perfect doll—the loveliest, daintiest, most ladylike doll she had ever seen. "Oh," she said softly. She had never wanted anything so much, so suddenly. In the picture the doll stood with her hands by her sides, her head tilted slightly. She had a soft smile that seemed to ask Ruthie to love her.

"Look," she said. For an instant she forgot how she hated her brothers. She pushed the catalog across the table and read from the description beside the doll. "It says, 'a beautifully tinted extra-fine bisque head.' Doesn't that sound elegant? And she's got moving eyelids—and Mother, she's wearing a cashmere coat! And lace on her underwear!"

Mother looked up from her work and smiled.

"Why would you want a doll like that?" Paul

asked. "You don't know anybody with lace on their underwear."

"I like dolls," Ruthie said. "I love this one."

"You never play with dolls."

"I would if I had this one. I would play with it all the time, and you boys would not be allowed to touch it ever."

Ruthie could imagine having such a doll. She would brush its long dark curls. She would sing it to sleep. Unlike Bert, her doll would never holler, burp, or smell bad. She would make beautiful dresses for it and take it for walks by the river. She would name it something wondrously elegant, like Clarinda.

"If I had a doll like this, I could be a lady," Ruthie said.

Ted burst out laughing, but no one else did. Joe looked up at Mother, who was setting bread dough for the morning.

Mother cleared her throat. "How much does that doll cost?" she asked.

Ruthie bit her lip. "Four ninety-five."

"Nearly five dollars," Mother said. Ruthie nodded. A new boughten dress could be had for a dollar. A kitchen cabinet like the one Mother wanted cost less than ten dollars.

"Well, then," Mother said briskly, "it looks like you'll have to be a lady on your own."

Ruthie nodded. Clarinda might as well have cost a hundred dollars. They could never spend that much for a toy.

12

Praying for Peace

W ednesday nights there was prayer meeting at church. Father often went, and
sometimes Ruthie did, too. They always walked,
to save the horses. Ruthie didn't like prayer
meetings as much as she liked walking through
the quiet evenings alone with her father. He
often let her carry the lantern.

One cold night just after Thanksgiving, Father
was silent the whole way to church. Ruthie's
boots crunched through the new snow, and the
lantern's bobbing light cast blue shadows on it.
Father seemed wrapped in thoughts of his own.
Ruthie didn't trouble him. She thought of Clarinda. She was going to save all her money until

she had enough. So far she had six cents, but she would find a way to earn more. She would buy Clarinda and become a lady the way Mother wanted. Hallie and Mallie would be her friends again. Already she had made a petticoat that would just suit Clarinda. Dottie was wearing it for now.

When the meeting was over and they were walking back along the dark road, Ruthie slipped her mittened hand inside her father's. "Why did we pray for peace tonight?" she asked. "Why do we always pray for it at supper now?"

Father looked grave. "Because of the war. No one wishes for war."

"But there is no war," Ruthie said.

Father said, "You know better. I see you read the papers every week."

There had been a war in Europe for a very long time. All the small countries were fighting each other. Germany against France and England. Ruthie didn't understand it much. Father said the countries in Europe were small like the states in America. Ruthie didn't see the point of Indiana attacking Ohio or Illinois.

"But that war is very far away from here," Ruthie said.

"Not far enough," Father said. "Some people think we should enter it, on England and France's side. Other people think it is not our fight. Everyone argues about it." He tightened his grip on Ruthie's fingers and smiled down at her. "All the grown-ups do. We worry about it, and so we pray for peace."

Ruthie remembered that Joe was worried, too. "What do you think?" Ruthie's voice was muffled by her scarf. "Do you think we should fight?"

"I think we must defend the side of right," Father answered. "It is our duty. At the same time, I don't have enough sons that I can bear to lose any of them."

It took Ruthie several moments to understand what he meant. "But our boys are too young to fight," she said.

"Joe will be sixteen this spring. Wars can last a long time."

"But he would never go away!"

Father smiled. "Oh, of course he would. A fine boy like Joe! But I may think of an honorable way to keep him from fighting. Don't worry. It's not time to worry yet. What were you thinking about on the way to the meeting? Your face was so solemn."

"Clarinda." Ruthie loved to say the name.

"Someone at school?"

"No." Ruthie was shocked by his ignorance. "She's the doll in the Sears catalog. I'm going to buy her when I get five dollars."

"I see." Father sounded amused. "And how will you get five dollars?"

"I'll find a way. I have several plans."

Father's laugh rang out like a bell through the cold night. "Ruthie," he said, "the Huns in Germany should be glad they're not fighting you."

13

Auditions!

One morning Mr. Ames made an announcement. "The school Christmas pageant will take place in three weeks, on Christmas Eve," he said. "Everyone will participate, but this year I am not going to assign the principal parts, as I have in the past. We will have auditions instead, on Wednesday, during the noon hour."

Ruthie's face lit up. Auditions! That meant she had a chance. Last year, as a lowly second-grader, she had been a sheep. Paul had been a shepherd, and so had Ted. Joe, the tallest boy in the school, had had to be Saint Joseph, Jesus's father. Ted would have liked the part, but Joe hated it. He was shy in large crowds. He had spoken his lines in a whisper, though he knew them perfectly by heart.

"Perhaps you can be Mary," Ruthie whispered to her seatmate, Mary. Mary's eyes widened and she shook her head. Ruthie grinned. She had only been teasing. Mary was quiet as a mouse. She would make a perfect sheep.

Ruthie knew what part she wanted. She would be the angel Gabriel, the herald of the Lord.

At home Ruthie read the Bible. Over and over she repeated the words of the angel. Mother listened and said she had done well. The boys hooted.

"You can't be an angel," Ted said. "You're not tall enough. Angels are supposed to be tall and beautiful. You're middling and plain."

"I'm still almost as tall as Paul," Ruthie retorted. "I'm prettier than any of you, except Bert." Bert was becoming a beautiful baby. His face was no longer red, and his blond hair curled.

"I don't want to be the angel," Paul answered. "I want to be a wise man. Wise men can be short."

Ted thought this was funny, too. Ruthie and Paul exchanged sympathetic looks. They were nearly back to being friends. "I'll stick to being a shepherd, thanks," Ted said. "You two can be the performers in the family."

"Perhaps I'll be asked to sing a song," said Ruthie.

Joe smiled at her. "Look, sis, don't pin too much hope on this," he said quietly. "Mr. Ames gives the big parts to the big kids. He always has."

Ruthie brushed his words aside. Perhaps she would be asked to sing. Perhaps she would sing very well. She could take to performing, and sing in Fort Wayne—in front of choirs, perhaps. People would pay to hear her, and she would buy Clarinda. It was possible.

She struck a dramatic pose in the farmhouse kitchen. " 'O-oh tidings of comfort and joy, comfort and joy,' " she sang. Ted covered his ears. In

75

the yard, one of the dogs howled. The boys howled with laughter. Ruthie blushed furiously, but she held her tongue. She'd show them. She would.

On Wednesday morning Ruthie was almost too nervous to eat breakfast. She waited at the end of the lane for Hallie and Mallie. "Aren't you excited?" she asked when she saw them.

"About what?" asked Mallie.

"The auditions!" Ruthie couldn't believe it. She'd been thinking of nothing else.

"We're not going to audition," Hallie said. "The real parts will go to the big girls. Plus they don't have any parts that both of us could do together."

"You could be the donkey," Ruthie suggested without thinking. Hallie gave her a sour look. Ruthie wished she'd held her tongue. She was trying so to win back their friendship, and sometimes they did play together at recess, but not often. They still hadn't forgiven her for the apple or the horror of Paul's crushed hand. Usually she ate her lunch alone.

Outside the schoolhouse a spotted horse stood tied behind a small black buggy, munching a nosebag of oats. Ruthie recognized the horse the moment she saw it. "The nurse is here," she said.

Hallie frowned. "What nurse?"

"Something about public health," Ruthie answered. "She came last year. She lined us all up and took our weights and heights and ages, and looked at our teeth, and asked if we ate vegetables and stuff." Ruthie remembered something else. Before the lady nurse measured them, she made them take off their boots. Ruthie looked at Hallie's and Mallie's stockings. They were the same black ones they usually wore—the made-over ones, without feet.

Hallie understood Ruthie's look. "I'm so embarrassed I'm going to die," she declared. She marched into the schoolroom. Mallie followed. Ruthie watched them go. She had to do something, or Hallie and Mallie would be shamed before the entire school.

14

Great Tidings of Glad Joy

❧

*R*uthie went around back to the privy. She unbuttoned her boots, took off her stockings, rolled them up, and hid them in her lunch pail. She pulled the legs of her long winter underwear down so that they tucked into the tops of her boots. Then she took her seat in the classroom.

Mr. Ames had them line up by age, just like last year. Ruthie pushed herself ahead of Hallie and Mallie. If everyone was going to laugh at Hallie and Mallie, they were going to have to laugh at her too. It wasn't a great plan, but it was the best she could think of so quickly.

"Take off your shoes, dear," the nurse said to

Ruthie. Ruthie pulled her boots off. The entire school saw her bare feet.

In summer everyone went barefoot all the time. But no one ever wore boots without stockings. Ruthie's feet were already cold.

The nurse seemed startled. "Where are your stockings?" she asked.

"I don't have any," Ruthie said loudly. "We're too poor."

The nurse looked at Ruthie's neat sweater and wool skirt. She looked at Ruthie's nearly new boots. She didn't seem to know what to say.

"That's a lie!" Paul said, equally loudly, from his place in line. "We are not poor. Ruthie, where are your stockings?"

"Shut up," Ruthie said. To the nurse she said, "That's my stupid brother. He doesn't know anything."

"Order!" Mr. Ames rapped his ruler on one of the empty desks. "Ruthie, when the nurse is finished with you, report to me." He sat down behind his desk, looking annoyed.

When Ruthie stood before him, her boots back on her naked feet, he looked at her for a long time before he spoke. When he did, his voice was low. Ruthie could feel the other students staring. No one was watching the nurse measure Hallie. No one was looking at Hallie's stockings.

"What was the purpose behind that display?" Mr. Ames asked.

"No purpose," Ruthie said. "Sir."

There was a pause. Mr. Ames looked gravely displeased. "I'll ask you again," he said. "I require an answer."

Ruthie turned and looked at the line of students across the room. Joe seemed perplexed, Paul furious, and Maude and Rosemarie disgusted. Everyone else, including Ted, looked amused. Mallie was using the nurse's hook to button her boots. She stood up and looked gratefully at Ruthie.

"I thought it would be a good joke," Ruthie said to Mr. Ames.

He turned toward Mallie for a moment and looked thoughtful. "Take your seat," he said to Ruthie. "During recess you will stay inside and write, one hundred times, 'I will show respect for my classmates by my dress, words, and deeds.'"

"But I'll be auditioning then," Ruthie protested.

Mr. Ames raised his eyebrows. "You may write during the time that the audition does not require," he said. "If you do not finish, you may stay after school to complete your punishment." Ruthie nodded and started back to her seat.

"Ruthie," he continued, "if you could miraculously afford stockings by tomorrow, I would appreciate it."

"Yes, sir," Ruthie said. She certainly could. Her boots rubbed her toes.

Midmorning, when the nurse was gone and the recitations had begun, Hallie slid a folded note across the aisle. Ruthie opened it with trembling fingers. It read, "Do you want to jump rope today?"

Ruthie turned it over. "I can't," she wrote, cupping her hand over the paper so Mr. Ames wouldn't see. "I have auditions. But I will tomorrow."

Hallie read it, smiled, and nodded. Ruthie felt

filled with great contentment. Hallie and Mallie had forgiven her.

At noontime she strode to the front of the classroom, planted her feet, and tossed back her head. " 'Fear not,' " she proclaimed, looking boldly around the schoolhouse, " 'for behold, I bring you great tidings of glad joy, which shall be unto all people!' "

15

Tattletales

After school the storm broke. First Maude said that Ruthie was the worst show-off she had ever seen, bar none. "And vulgar, too," she continued, in front of a gathering crowd. "Imagine, not wearing stockings! You're like a wild animal."

Hallie marched up to Maude. "Take that back right now," she said, "or my sister and I will never play with you again."

"I don't care," said Maude.

"Fine." Hallie linked arms with Ruthie on one side and Mallie on the other. They walked home together with their heads high. None of them said a word about the stockings.

But when Ruthie walked into the kitchen she found all the boys gathered there. From the way they fell silent she knew they had been telling Mother about it. Mother's face was tight-lipped and furious.

"Tattletales!" Ruthie shrieked.

Ted laughed. "Go get 'em, sis," he said. "But don't blame me. I didn't tell." He grabbed an apple and ran up the stairs.

"Sorry, Ruthie," Joe began awkwardly. "But you shouldn't have—"

"You told everyone we were too poor to buy stockings!" Paul shouted. He looked angry as a hen in a rainstorm. "You know that's not true! We've got just as much money as anyone else in Cedarville!"

Ruthie couldn't imagine why Paul cared. The whole school, including Mr. Ames, knew they weren't dirt-poor. Only the nurse wouldn't know different, and she didn't matter.

"Explain yourself," Mother ordered.

"I . . . I can't," Ruthie said. She'd kept Hallie

and Mallie's secret this long. She couldn't betray it now.

"*Ruth Ann Hawk.*" Mother's voice was like thunder.

Ruthie twisted the edge of her sweater in her hands. "Not in front of them," she pleaded.

Mother glanced sideways. Joe got up immediately. Paul looked inclined to stay, but Joe caught him by the collar and hauled him out the door. As soon as they were gone, Ruthie confessed everything.

Mother's face grew calmer and calmer. By the time Ruthie was finished, she didn't seem angry at all, but she looked at Ruthie with a sorrowful expression.

"I know I wasn't a lady," Ruthie said.

"No, you weren't," Mother agreed. "Your intentions were honorable, and your actions were noble, but no one could call them genteel."

"If I could have thought of something better, I'd have done it," Ruthie said. "Am I in trouble?"

"Not as much trouble as you might have been,"

Mother answered. "I'm glad you wanted to help your friends. However, I can't have you acting so disrespectful in school." She disappeared into the parlor and came back with a large hank of wool yarn and a set of double-pointed knitting needles. "Here's your punishment. You may not play outside or have company after school, until you've knitted three pairs of stockings."

"Three pairs?" Ruthie was aghast. She was not a speedy knitter. Stockings took her ages.

"Yes," Mother said firmly. "Three pairs, tightly knit and with turned heels. One for you, one for Hallie, and one for Mallie. It might be nice if you finished by Christmas."

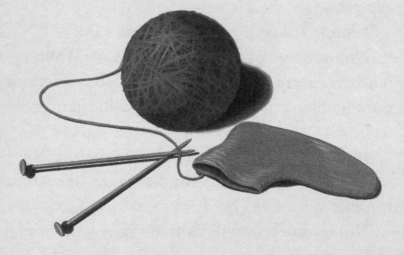

Nice! It would be a Christmas miracle. Ruthie took the needles and glumly started to cast on the yarn. She was sorry to be punished and sorrier still to have disappointed Mother again. But as she looped the yarn over and around the needle, a small warm feeling stayed steady in her heart.

She was not sorry for what she'd done. Not at all.

Next morning they arrived at school to find that Mr. Ames had written the pageant parts on the blackboard. "The angel—Ruth Hawk." Ruthie stared and stared. Never before had her name looked beautiful.

16

Sick, Sleepy Angel

❧

There were only two weeks until Christmas. The old snow melted into tired heaps, and the air grew cold and damp; the clouds seemed to hang just above the earth, waiting. Dark came so early that the boys had to light lanterns in the barn, and Ruthie hastened with the chickens after school so that she was finished before they started to roost.

Every day while she was doing her chores, helping Mother with Bert, studying her schoolbooks, or knitting Hallie's and Mallie's stockings, the words of the angel crowded into Ruthie's head. "Fear not," she whispered. She imagined herself on Christmas Eve, standing in the center of the stage in front of the entire town. "Fear not!" she would say, and everyone would watch her, and listen.

In the evenings Father read the paper with a furrowed brow. Ruthie saw that the headlines spoke of the faraway war. Sometimes she saw Joe looking anxiously at Father. "Fear not!" she whispered to Joe then.

The week before Christmas, Ruthie began to feel a heaviness in her chest. Her nose ran and her ears felt plugged; worse yet, her lungs were so full and heavy she could hardly breathe. When she practiced her part, "Fear not" came out "Fear nob" and she couldn't declaim the words without falling into a coughing fit. She didn't say anything to anyone. Bert was fussy from teething every night, Aunt Cleone had gone home, and Mother never slept enough. She didn't notice Ruthie's cough. Ruthie hid it from the others as much as she could.

"You're sick," Paul accused her one morning as Ruthie struggled to put her coat on without coughing again.

"I am not," she said fiercely.

"Look at you!" Paul scowled. "Your eyes look funny. And we all heard you coughing last night. You kept us awake. I'm telling Mother."

Ruthie turned on him. "The way you told her about my stockings? The way you told her about my being tardy? The way you tell her everything? You are the worst tattletaling sneak in the entire world!" She coughed hard.

Paul looked stung. "But you're sick! You shouldn't go to school. It's snowing outside. You'll get wet."

Ruthie looked out the window. Snowflakes were drifting quietly to the ground. "If I'm sick, they won't let me be the angel." She coughed. "I'm not sick. I'm not. I won't be."

Paul stuck his hands in his pockets. Ruthie stared at him. "You're going to be a fine angel," he said at last.

Ruthie nodded. "You tell all those boys to leave me be. I feel fine."

He nodded. "Okay."

But by noon that day Ruthie could no longer pretend to be well. The snow continued, and at recess all the students had a wild snowball fight, but she stayed inside, huddled next to the stove to keep warm. She coughed and shook. Mr. Ames hovered over her.

"I'd send you home now, but I don't want you walking alone through the snow. Can you last until four, or should I have your brother Joe take you?"

"I'm fine," Ruthie insisted through chattering teeth. "I don't feel bad at all. I'll be much better tomorrow." She had never felt so poorly in her life.

Mr. Ames watched her for a long moment. "I'll call Joe," he said. He walked toward the door.

"Mr. Ames!" He turned. "Please don't let Maude be the angel."

He smiled. "All right, Ruthie. I give you my word."

Joe piggybacked her home. Before Ruthie knew it she was tucked up in her bed, snug beneath extra quilts, with a thick square of flannel against her chest. Mother brought her sweet weak tea and fed her from a spoon. "I'll be better very soon," Ruthie said. "I'll be fine in time for the pageant."

She drifted into sleep, and seemed to sleep a very long time. She felt cold, then hot, then cold again. Someone put a wet cloth against her forehead. Sometimes she coughed. Once she heard her mother singing, and once she felt a sharp pain against her side, but she was too sleepy to move or cry out. Then she heard voices: a thick, unfamiliar one, and her mother, crying. She tried to open her eyes, but she was so tired. She went back to sleep.

Ruthie opened her eyes. It was morning; bright winter sunlight streamed through the window. She couldn't understand why she hadn't been called for breakfast. It must be past eight o'clock. She was late for school.

She hurried to get up, but her head felt heavy, and when she lifted it off the pillow the room swam dizzily around her. She lay back down. Her room looked different. The trundle bed was gone, and Bert's cradle sat in its place. Mother's rocking chair had been brought up from the par-

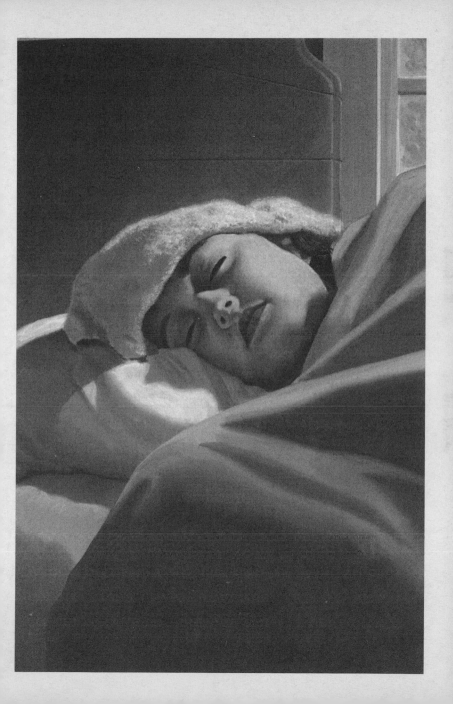

lor. On Ruthie's bedside table, a glass of water sat beside Mother's knitting and a big wooden bowl. Ruthie frowned. Why was Mother's knitting in her bedroom? She reached for the water, but it had frozen in the glass. She put it back and wished the walls would stop spinning so.

The door creaked open. Paul looked in, and his eyes widened. "Ruthie!" he yelled.

"Hello, Paul," Ruthie whispered. Paul was already gone; she could hear his footsteps pounding down the stairs.

"Mother, Mother! She's awake!"

For some reason Paul's cry raised a lot of people: Paul, Mother (with Bert), Father, Charlie, Luther, Aunt Cleone, and even Grandma Hawk, who lived in town, all crowded into Ruthie's bedroom. They grinned at her and asked how she felt. Even the little boys stared at her, including Bert.

"I'm okay," Ruthie answered doubtfully. "I'm fine. Why didn't you wake me up for school? Why didn't Paul go?"

Mother had tears in her eyes. She brushed Ruthie's hair back from her forehead and kissed her tenderly. "Darling," she said, "you've been sick a long time."

Ruthie didn't understand. "I'm thirsty," she said.

"I'll get you some water, dear." Aunt Cleone rushed from the room. Ruthie was amazed. No one had ever rushed to get her anything before. When Aunt Cleone came back with a fresh glass of water, everyone watched Ruthie drink.

"Do you all have to keep looking at me?" she asked. Everyone laughed, as though she had said something funny.

"Guess I'll go out to the barn, then," Ruthie's father announced. "Ruthie, I'll come up and see you again soon."

Father left whistling. Ruthie was more and more confused. Her mother kept patting her, touching her. This was not how Mother acted.

Grandma Hawk gave Ruthie's mother a long hug. This was not how Ruthie's grandmother usually acted, either. "You sit right down next to her and nurse Bert," Grandma directed, pushing Mother into the rocking chair. "You just watch her. I know how it is. I'll make us all some tea."

She and Aunt Cleone herded the boys out of the room, and Ruthie was left with her mother and little Bert, who looked hungry and also bigger than usual.

Ruthie sank her head into her feather pillow. Suddenly she felt tired again. "I'm sleepy," she said.

"That's fine. Go on to sleep." Mother rubbed her back.

"What happened?" Ruthie asked.

Mother didn't say anything for a long time. Ruthie drifted toward sleep. "Your brother saved your life," Mother said at last.

"Which one?" Ruthie asked drowsily. Her thinking still seemed very confused, but her pillow felt so soft. She shut her eyes.

Mother understood. "Paul."

17

A Train Just for Ruthie

When Ruthie woke again, it was a little later the same day. As soon as she opened her eyes she saw Paul grinning back at her. "They said you were better," he announced.

"I guess so," Ruthie said.

"Mother made broth, and if you drink it all, you can open your Christmas stocking. That's what she said. I can only stay with you a few minutes. I'm not allowed to tire you."

Paul handed her a mug full of hot chicken broth. Ruthie sat up a little and carefully sipped it. The walls of the room weren't spinning as much. "What do you mean, I can open my

Christmas stocking?" she asked. "Santa Claus hasn't come yet."

Paul stared. "Ruthie," he said softly, "it's the seventh of January."

Ruthie stared back.

"You've been sick a long time," Paul said.

"I'm nine years old," Ruthie said. "I slept through my birthday! And Christmas! And I didn't get to be the angel, either!" She sat up straight and the walls swirled. She leaned back against the pillows. "It's not fair!"

Paul sat down on the foot of the bed. "Mother didn't make your birthday cake yet. She said she was waiting until you could eat it. And nobody got to be the angel."

"What do you mean?"

Paul leaned his back against the footboard and grinned. "Remember the snow the day Joe took you home? It didn't quit snowing for five days. The roads were blocked, so everybody had to stay home on Christmas Eve, and they canceled the pageant. I reckon you can be the angel next year." His voice softened. "We all thought you were going to be a real angel, instead. Everybody except Mother thought you were certain to die."

Ruthie regarded him skeptically. "Mother said you saved my life."

Paul looked sheepish. "I didn't do much. I just got the train here, that's all."

"What train?"

"See, the doctor couldn't get here because of the snow. But you were so bad, and nobody knew what to do—I told them, but they didn't really listen, Mother and Father were so worried about you. So I just went into town to the train station, and they telegraphed to Fort Wayne, and the station man there found the doctor and sent him here on a train. Only think of it, Ruthie! A whole train, just for you!" Paul's eyes shone.

"You walked to town in a blizzard by yourself," Ruthie said.

"Wasn't much. I only got a little frostbitten. It was cold. The doctor thought so, too."

"And you saved my life," Ruthie said. The words sounded strange. She didn't like being beholden to Paul, but she was awfully glad to be alive.

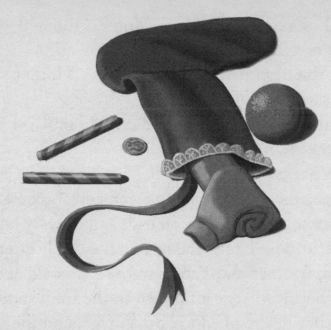

"I don't know," Paul said. "I think it was Mother who saved you. You just got worse and worse, and she wouldn't let go of you. Not until the moment the doctor walked into the room. She . . . she held on to your life with both her hands. Doctor said he couldn't believe you'd lasted so long."

Ruthie stared. "I don't want any more broth," she said.

"Give it to me, I'll drink it. That way you can

open your stocking. Does your side hurt? The doctor cut you open. He said you had poison in your lung."

Ruthie felt along her side. She was wearing some sort of bandage. "I thought it was just my underwear itching."

Paul shook his head. "Doctor stuck a knife in you, right here in this bedroom. Don't look so queasy. I guess I'm glad he did it."

"I guess I am, too."

Inside Ruthie's stocking were a rolled pair of new machine-knit stockings, a new set of winter underwear, two peppermint sticks, a green hair ribbon, an orange, and, in the very toe, a silver dime. Ruthie spread the riches across her top quilt. "Look at all this!" she said. "A whole dime!" She had never had so much money all at once. "I'll save it for Clarinda," she said. Now she had sixteen cents. She only needed four hundred and seventy-nine more.

"We kept your orange from freezing," Paul said. "It wasn't easy, the house got so cold."

Ruthie stacked the stockings, underwear, and ribbon neatly on her bedside table. She set her orange and dime next to them. "We can each have a peppermint stick," she said.

Paul took the one she offered. "It's good to have you back," he said.

"I'm sorry I ever called you a sneak," Ruthie said.

Paul shrugged. "I'm sorry I ever was one."

18

The Pickle Jar

*I*t was ages before Ruthie was truly well. The doctor came several more times, though not on a train or through a snowstorm. He examined the wound on Ruthie's side and listened carefully to her breathing. He said her lungs were still weak. He advised caution and moderation.

Ruthie thought she would rather be dead than spend a single minute more in her bed. She whined until Mother was tired of listening.

"Ladies don't complain," Mother said sharply.

"Do ladies die of pneumonia?" Ruthie asked.

"No," said Mother. "Nor did you." But she took the rocking chair back downstairs to the

kitchen, and Father carried Ruthie down to it
every morning. While Mother cooked and did
laundry, Ruthie rocked Bert or tossed a yarn ball
to Charlie. Sometimes she tied her new ribbon in
Bert's hair.

"Please can't we pretend he's a girl?" she asked.
"Can't we call him Bertha?"

"No," Mother said. "I already told you."

"He's too young to care."

"Bertha," Charlie said clearly. He was talking
well now. He giggled. Ruthie giggled back.

"I would care," Mother replied. "Imagine if
we'd pretended you were a boy! It's wrong. You
are what you are." Mother stirred the stew she
was making for supper.

"I'm not a lady," Ruthie said sadly. She rocked
and rocked. Bert cooed and played with the ends
of her braids. There was a spot on the ceiling
shaped just like a rooster. Outside, the fields were
boring, covered with snow. The boys had made a
snowman where Ruthie could see it from the
kitchen window. Now they were playing Fox and
Geese in the far pasture. Ruthie loved Fox and
Geese.

"You will be one," Mother assured her. "It's simply a matter of application."

"What does that mean?"

"It means when you try hard enough, it will happen."

"But I'm trying hard now!" Ruthie said. "If I had a doll like Clarinda, it would be easier. Having her would be almost like having a sister. It's going to be a long time before I can save up forty-eight more dimes."

Mother turned from the stove. She wiped her hand on her apron. "If I had forty-nine dimes to spare, I would buy you Clarinda myself," she said. "I would have loved to have a doll like that when I was your age." She began peeling potatoes.

Ruthie rocked silently. She hadn't thought her mother would understand. "I expect I might find a job this summer," she said at last. "I'll save up."

Mother smiled but shook her head sadly. Ruthie knew what that meant. Who would hire a nine-year-old girl when they might hire Joe or Ted or even Paul instead? "I could watch someone's babies for them."

"I'm not letting you travel into town for work," Mother said firmly. "You're too young for that. Besides, I shall need you here to help me with Bert, and to pick the strawberries. You know that."

"And the hens," Ruthie said, looking at the rooster shape on the ceiling.

"And the hens. Poor hens, they miss you."

Ruthie looked down at her lap. Bert had fallen asleep. She called to her mother to take him, and then she picked her sewing up from the floor. She had finished the eternal stockings, although she hadn't been allowed to see Hallie and Mallie yet, and now she was making a tiny skirt out of a scrap left over from last year's Sunday dress.

"What are you sewing?" Mother asked. Ruthie held it up.

"You're doing well. You've become more patient, Ruthie."

"It's for Clarinda," Ruthie explained. "When I get her I shall want her nicely dressed."

Mother turned from laying Bert in his basket. She looked at Ruthie for a long time.

"You said I could have the fabric," Ruthie said.

Mother walked briskly to the pantry and came back with an empty pickle jar. She handed it to Ruthie, went into her bedroom, and came back with her pocketbook. She dropped a nickel into the jar. "We'll save it from the housekeeping," she declared. "We'll get you that doll."

19

Surprises

❧

*R*uthie added her sixteen cents to the jar, so right away they had twenty-one. Mother put the jar back on the pantry shelf. Every week she added another nickel or sometimes a dime; once, when Father sold the yearling colt, she added a whole quarter. Mother let Ruthie's last year's spring dress down and said it would have to do for this year, and she planned to make new spring trousers only for Ted, who needed them most, but she still saved for Clarinda. Every Saturday when she added another coin she let Ruthie count the money in the jar.

In mid-February Paul came home from school grinning wildly. "Ready?" he asked Mother.

Mother grinned back. "Ready," she said.

"What for?" asked Ruthie. She was improving steadily. She was able to walk a few steps now.

"Surprise!" Hallie and Mallie burst into the kitchen. They threw their arms around Ruthie, who was so glad to see them that she had to sit back down.

"I missed you," she said.

"We wanted to come earlier," Hallie said. "No one would let us. They said you were too sick."

"We have a present for you," Mallie added. She had a basket over her arm.

Mother took their wraps and handed around milk and cookies. Ruthie knew she must be a polite hostess, but she was dying to know what was in that basket.

"I have presents for you, too," she said. She dug the stockings out of the bottom of her sewing basket. Mother had given her a bit of paper to wrap them in. "They were meant for Christmas," she said.

Hallie and Mallie unwrapped the stockings.

For a moment Ruthie was afraid they would feel too proud to accept them.

"Glory be!" Hallie said. "Can you show us how to make them?"

"Of course," Ruthie said. She smiled at her mother. "Come every day after school, and I'll teach you."

The basket made a murmuring noise. Mallie opened it and pulled out a kitten. "Our mama cat had another litter," she said. "We picked out the nicest one for you. It's a girl." The kitten was a

wee gray thing, with fur soft as goose down and tiny claws like milkweed thistles.

Ruthie cradled her in her arms. "I'll call her Priscilla," she said. It was the second most elegant name she knew.

"That's almost as nice as Clarinda," Hallie said approvingly.

"You couldn't name a cat Clarinda." Mallie sounded shocked.

"Why not?" Hallie asked.

Ruthie fetched one of Clarinda's petticoats and tried to fasten it around Priscilla's waist. Priscilla twisted out of it.

"You just couldn't," Mallie said. "It's a special name."

Ruthie told Hallie and Mallie about the jar of coins saved for Clarinda. The twins' eyes opened wide. "That's glorious," Mallie said. "You'll have her by next Christmas."

Ruthie grinned. "Maybe even before."

Mother let Ruthie keep Priscilla, but only outside, in the barn. "But it's too cold and she's so little," Ruthie protested. "Couldn't we just once have a house cat?"

"She'll be plenty warm in the barn," Mother said firmly.

"But I'm not allowed outside," Ruthie said. "She'll forget who I am."

Mother sighed. She allowed Priscilla inside the house to sit on Ruthie's lap for a half hour each day. "The first time I find cat hair in my pantry, she stays in the barn for good," Mother warned.

"She's a very good cat," Luther said, sticking up for Priscilla. He caught her in the loft every day and brought her in to Ruthie. Luther was useful for running other errands, too, such as fetching Ruthie's sewing scraps or bringing her a drink of water. Ruthie had almost gotten so that she didn't mind him hanging around.

After their first visit Hallie and Mallie came several times a week. Sometimes Mrs. Graber and baby Sarah came too, and when they did, Mrs. Graber and Ruthie's mother would sit in the parlor and the girls would have the kitchen all to themselves. They would knit and talk. The twins' stockings were progressing rapidly. As Mallie said, they were highly motivated.

"We're going to throw those wretched hand-me-downs into the stove," she declared.

"What's happening at school?" Ruthie asked. She was surprised to find that she missed it some. She was so bored with sitting at home.

"Maude and Alice have formed a club," Hallie said. "Maude is president."

Ruthie sniffed. "I wouldn't be in any club of theirs," she said.

"Nor would we," Mallie assured her. "Can you imagine? She asked us!"

Hallie looked fierce. "Only so she could have somebody to boss. Maude is president, Alice is vice president, and Rosemarie is secretary. They don't have anyone left for regular members."

"What do they do?" Ruthie asked.

"Nothing," said Hallie.

"They wear badges to school and whisper to each other," Mallie said. "That's all. And all the boys are playing Frogs and Huns."

It sounded like Fox and Geese. "It's a war game," Mallie explained. "They're playing war. Everybody is talking about fighting in the war."

Ruthie nodded. Her parents never spoke of it to her, but sometimes she overheard them talking to each other. "Does Joe play?" she asked.

"No-o-o," said Hallie. "Ted does. And Paul."

"Joe's afraid he'll have to fight," Ruthie explained.

"He's not grown!" protested Mallie.

"Our uncle is joining the army," Hallie said. "If there is a war, he's going to fight."

Mallie made a face at her knitting. "Mother worries," she whispered. "He's her only brother."

Before Bert was born, Ruthie would have said that having six brothers was definitely worse than having five. Now she didn't think so. Which one could she spare?

20

The Center of Attention

❧

*I*n late March Ruthie finally returned to school. Father hitched the team to the wagon and drove her in, to spare her the walk. She sat on the seat while the boys and Hallie and Mallie crowded in the back. They attracted some notice when they pulled up in front of the school. The other pupils stopped their play, and Mr. Ames came out to greet them. He shook hands with Father and helped Ruthie down. "We're pleased to have you back, Ruth," he said. "The third grade was a little thin without you."

Ruthie grinned at him. "At least it didn't disappear," she said.

To her surprise, he grinned too. "We were spared that calamity," he said. "Shall I help you inside?"

Ruthie shook her head. "No, thank you, please." She wanted to look around a bit by herself. After the isolation of the farmhouse, the town seemed almost overstimulating. Across the street a freight wagon pulled up at the train station. A horse whinnied loudly. One of the merchants was sweeping his stoop.

Father tipped his hat to her and drove off, but Hallie, Mallie, and her brothers hovered near her. "I'm not going to faint or fall down," she told them.

"You're not moving," Paul said. "Are your feet stuck?"

"I'm taking my time," she said. *"Shorty."* Because a strange thing had happened. While she was ill, she had grown two inches. She was taller than Paul again.

Paul stuck out his tongue, which made her glad. At least it was what she expected.

"C'mon, sis," said Ted. "We've got to get you inside. Can't have the air giving you a chill."

She had to guard against chills until her lungs were stronger. Still, their solicitude amazed her. "I'm fine," she snapped. "Why are you fussing over me?"

Joe's expression turned sad so fleetingly that Ruthie wondered if she had imagined it. "You're the only sister we've got," he said. He bent down and swooped her into his arms. Paul and Ted took her lunch pail and books, and they paraded into the schoolhouse, Hallie and Mallie following behind.

Joe sat her down at her desk. Ruthie actually was grateful. Her legs were still a little unsteady, and she wasn't used to being outside. She remembered how Joe had piggybacked her home before Christmas. "You carried me out and now you're carrying me in," she told him.

"Always at your service," Joe replied.

"Oh, Joe," she whispered, "please don't leave us."

"What are you two on about?" Ted asked, interrupting Joe's reply. Ruthie wished he hadn't. What would Joe have said?

Mary, her seatmate, brought her a daffodil

from the ones growing around the privy. "Don't think about where it came from, just think about how pretty it looks," she instructed Ruthie. In three months, Mary seemed to have gotten a great deal older. She had been too shy to say much to Ruthie before.

"I'm glad you're back," Mary continued. "I missed the drawings on your slate."

Whenever Ruthie was angry, she drew pictures of her brothers or the fourth-graders dying horrible deaths. Now, for Mary's benefit, she drew a picture of Mary with flowers in her hands.

She was far behind in her lessons, but no one seemed concerned. Mr. Ames told her to join in where Hallie and Mallie were studying. Over the summer she could read the work she'd missed.

At recess the girls crowded around Ruthie's desk. The doctor had told her that she couldn't play outside for another few weeks, at least. Ruthie was surprised to be the center of attention. Even Maude, Rosemarie, and Alice sat down and said hello. They all wore badges, just as Hallie had said, and Maude fingered hers while she spoke.

"We've made a club," she said.

Ruthie swept her with a scornful glance. "I heard."

"Would you—"

"Hallie," Ruthie said, "tell Mary about your kittens."

On the way home in Father's wagon Hallie put her arm around Ruthie. "I'm glad you put Maude in her place," she said.

Ruthie was scornful. "Why would she talk to me about her stupid club anyway? I wouldn't even join the fourth grade because Maude was there."

"She thinks you're interesting now, since you almost died," Mallie explained.

"Well, I'm not. I'm just the same, and I don't believe she's changed a bit, either. She just didn't like to see everyone talking to me."

At home Ruthie told her mother about Maude. "I didn't hit her," she said. "I just ignored her. Was that the ladylike thing to do?"

Mother seemed startled by the question. "I don't know," she said. "I'm sure it's preferable to hitting."

"Oh." Ruthie had been so sure Mother would be proud.

21

Stampeded into War

❦

*O*n the first day of April, a Sunday, Mother's mare had a chestnut filly foal. Irises bloomed in the flower beds, and the ice on the river melted for good. In the evenings Ruthie read the newspaper anxiously. The headlines were getting worse. One long story started out, "We are being stampeded into this war."

"What does 'stampeded' mean?" she asked Father.

"You know that," he replied. "Run over by a herd of panicked, unthinking horses."

"Who are the horses?"

He shook his head. "Other countries. Politicians. But the trampled ones, the soldiers, will be like the people we know."

At school they talked of war in the classroom as well as in the yard. Mr. Ames brought in a map and showed them all of the small countries in Europe. He pointed out Germany, which was trying to take over the rest. Then he made a patriotic speech. "It is our sacred duty to fight," he declared.

Ruthie raised her hand.

"Yes, Ruthie?" he said.

"Why?"

Mr. Ames was more patient than annoyed. "When some nations are oppressing others—are doing bad things deliberately, and for their own gain—then the rest of the world must act to prevent it. When we see wrong being done, whether here in our village or elsewhere in the world, we must try to make it right."

Ruthie could see both sides. Germany was bossy, bullying, and rude, like Maude. It had to be put in its place. But soldiers died in wars, and if this one went on forever, Ted and even Paul might have to fight. Ruthie's great-uncle, Father's uncle, had died at the Battle of Bull Run, in the Civil War, when Ruthie's grandfather was but a small boy. It was no wonder Father dreaded sending Joe.

One thing was certain. She wouldn't have to go. Girls never fought wars.

"Do *you* think we should fight?" Ruthie asked Joe on the way home from school. She fell back a little so the others wouldn't listen, and he fell back in step with her.

His answer surprised her. "Yes, I do," he said. "I think the Germans are wrong. The United States has always stood for freedom, and we must stand for freedom now."

"But aren't you afraid to fight?"

Joe's face looked sad, as it so often did now. "Yes and no," he said. "I am afraid, but I don't think I'm any more afraid than anyone else. I'm not so afraid I wouldn't do it. But I'm not so eager to go that I'd lie to the conscriptors, either.

"We all do things we don't want to do," he continued. "Think about it, sis. You do all the time."

"That's because I'm a girl."

Joe shook his head. "No, it isn't. Not totally, anyway. If you were a boy, you'd just have different things you'd have to do."

Ruthie disagreed. She started to say so, but Joe stopped and bent over. "Look around," he said, making a sweeping motion with his arm. "Isn't this beautiful?"

Ruthie looked. It truly was. All along the riverbank, the trees were bursting with tiny pale green leaves. The redbuds were in bloom, and underneath the trees a profusion of spring wildflowers made white, pink, and yellow patches against the earth. The river ran high and clear. On the roadbed the grass looked like bright green velvet.

"I love it here," Joe said simply. "I'm not afraid to fight, but I dread having to leave."

Ruthie squeezed his hand tight. She understood. She didn't know what to say.

Within days Germany declared war on the United States, and at home that night Father said retaliation was inevitable.

"What does that mean?" Ruthie asked.

"It means we're going to fight back," he told her.

"But we have to!" Ted spoke up. Father was silent.

On Thursday, the fifth of April, the students had just settled into their desks after recess when they heard shouting in the street. Mr. Ames opened a window. A train had pulled up at the station. "Extra, extra!" Ruthie heard someone shout. The students ran to the door. A man was waving a newspaper from a bundle that had just come off the train. The headline was so large Ruthie could read it from the school window: "UNITED STATES AT WAR."

22

Trying to Be Brave

Mr. Ames dismissed the school. At home Father and Mother were sitting down, indoors, right in the middle of the day. "The House of Representatives has voted for war," Father told them. He had read the extra paper. "The Senate will vote tomorrow, and then we will be at war with Germany."

Mother began to cry.

Father put his arm around Joe and sent the rest of the children off to their chores. Ruthie tried to stay, but Mother put her out.

"Why is Mother crying?" Luther asked. They loitered in the yard.

Ruthie bent and hugged him. "They think

Joe'll have to fight," she said. "He'll go to Germany and maybe die."

Paul scowled. "I wouldn't mind going to Germany! I'd show those Huns! I wouldn't die!" He kicked the porch post.

"Joe would mind," Ruthie said. "You know that."

"Anyway, you're wrong," Ted declared. "He's too young. Only grown-ups fight."

"He won't have to go right away," Ruthie said. She took her comfort from that. But Joe was nearly grown. "Father told me wars last for years and years," she added reluctantly.

"Then I'll be grown, and I can fight," Paul said. "They can't have Joe. We need him here." He kicked the post again.

"You stupid boys!" Ruthie exclaimed. She went up to the hayloft to get away from them. She coaxed Priscilla into her lap and cuddled her. It began to rain, loud against the roof.

She made a pile of loose hay and snuggled into it, holding Priscilla tight against her chest. The kitten mewed. Ruthie fell asleep.

When she woke it was almost dark. The loft

was full of shadows. The rain still made a hard noise against the roof, and underneath that was a softer sound Ruthie first thought was her kitten. But Priscilla was asleep. Ruthie rubbed her eyes and looked around her. The noise was someone crying.

It was Joe. He was huddled behind some hay bales under the eaves, and when he saw Ruthie staring he wiped his eyes and tried to pretend nothing was wrong. "Got some dust in my eyes," he said.

"You're not going to Germany, are you?" she asked. "You're too young! Mallie said you have to be eighteen to sign up for the army."

Joe gulped and shook his head. "Not Germany," he said. "Philadelphia. I'm going to Philadelphia. Monday morning, on the train. I'm going to work in a factory for the war."

"Oh, Joe!" Ruthie rushed to him and hugged him fiercely. "Please don't go! Stay here with us!"

Joe trembled. "I don't have a choice," he said. "Father says I must, and I . . . I'm sure he's right. Father's cousin William works in a munitions factory, making bullets and such, and he told Father a long time ago that they could get me a job there if . . . if need be. Philadelphia is a great big city. They have lots of factories there. It's important work. War work."

"But you love the farm," Ruthie said. "And Father said he'd let you tend a section this summer. You don't have to fight yet. You can just stay here."

"I won't be gone long," Joe said soothingly. He sat her down gently beside him. "If I take this job, I'll be part of the war effort, an important part, but I'll never have to be a soldier. If I stay here until I'm eighteen, likely the factories will be full of workers. Folks will call me a coward then if I don't go and fight. I don't want that."

"But you said you weren't afraid to fight!" Ruthie was furious.

"I'm not. It's Father who doesn't want me to be a soldier. He wants me to make bullets. Until I'm twenty-one I have to do what he says."

That was the law, Ruthie knew. "The war will be over soon now that we're in it," she said. "Ted said the Americans could whip the Huns and be back in a day."

Joe snorted. "It'll last years. Haven't you read your history book? All wars do."

"But you just said you'd only be gone a little while!"

Joe laughed a little shakily. "I'm trying to be brave," he said. "Everyone in the country will have to be brave now." Another sob escaped him, and he pressed the back of his hand to his mouth. "I'll be stuck in a stinking factory all day. Can you imagine me in a big city? I look like a farmer. I talk like one and I dress like one. I am one. Fort Wayne seems too crowded and fussy a city to me. Do you think Philadelphia will seem much bigger?"

"Probably not," Ruthie said loyally, though she knew it would. Joe would be lost in Philadelphia. He had never met Cousin William. He would not be near his family or his friends. It would be worse than being the only girl, or being the entire third grade.

23

Travel Plans

The next day was Good Friday, so there was no school. Joe sat at the breakfast table, pale and resolute, discussing his travel plans with Father. He was leaving Monday morning. He was not even taking the Cedarville train; Father would drive him to the station in Fort Wayne. He would not go back to school or get to say good-bye to most of his friends.

Mother seemed hurried and distracted. When Charlie dropped his milk, she snapped at him. "Be careful!"

"It's not his fault!" Ruthie snapped back. She comforted Charlie.

"Go on, Ruthie, get to your work outside," Father said. Mother's expression looked dangerous. The rest of the boys had already fled to the barn. Ruthie followed, but she felt murderous. How could they send Joe away? She made hasty work of the chickens and headed for Hallie and Mallie's.

Mrs. Graber and the twins were making hot cross buns when Ruthie burst through the door. "Good morning, dear," Mrs. Graber said. "What's wrong?"

"My brother is going away!" Ruthie flung herself into a chair.

Hallie nibbled a piece of dough. "Joe?" she asked. Ruthie nodded.

"Maude's brother is signing up, too," Mallie said. "He's old enough, he's eighteen. Joe's not. Is he going to lie about his age?"

"He's going to a factory," Ruthie spat. "He's going to make guns."

"That's patriotic," Hallie said. "They'll need a lot of guns."

"It's horrible," Ruthie said. "Ted wants to go, too. He begged all night, but Mother won't let him. Joe's frightened. I'd go work in a factory if they'd let me, if they'd let Joe stay home. Ted and I could go."

"You'd be frightened, too," Mrs. Graber said gently.

"No, I wouldn't. Nothing ever frightens me."

To her surprise, Mrs. Graber bent and kissed her on the forehead. "I know. Now, what can we do to help Joe get ready?"

Ruthie had not thought of that. Hallie finished rolling out the buns and rinsed her hands in the sink. Mallie sat down beside Ruthie. "At school Mr. Ames said we will all learn how to knit," Mallie said. "Even the boys. We'll knit stockings for the soldiers."

"We can all knit stockings already," Ruthie said scornfully. "But I'm still not fast enough to knit a pair by Monday."

"I am," Mrs. Graber said. "So I'll do that."

Ruthie thought hard. "I've got a piece of silk Mother gave me to make Clarinda a skirt," she said. "I could hem that to make Joe a new handkerchief."

"That's a good idea," Mrs. Graber said approvingly.

"I'd like to make him a necktie, too, but I don't think there's enough silk." Ruthie swung her feet, frowning. "If we pieced it together—"

"We've got some," Hallie said. "That gray piece. We can make Joe a necktie out of that."

"But that was for your cats," Ruthie said. It was a fine square piece of figured silk, nearly a yard, and it was Hallie and Mallie's most prized possession.

"War is a time of sacrifice," Mallie said grandly.

Ruthie rocked Sarah while Mrs. Graber put the buns to rise on the back of the stove and Hallie and Mallie brought down their sewing baskets. They would all work on Joe's necktie. A handkerchief wouldn't take long; Ruthie could make it at home later.

Sarah reached up and grabbed Ruthie's braid. Ruthie gently took it back. "War is a time for sacrifice," she repeated to the baby. In Philadelphia Joe would be as out of place as a pig in church. She wondered what else she could do to help him fit in.

24

Sacrifice

❦

*T*hat night Ruthie crept back downstairs after Mother had sent them all to bed. In the living room Mother sat close to the big oil lamp, with all of Joe's clothes piled on a table nearby. She was mending every tear and ripped stitch. Father was in the barn; one of the cows was about to calve.

"Ruthie, go back upstairs," Mother commanded, without looking up from the shirt she was working on.

"I need a drink of water," Ruthie said.

"Be quick, then."

Ruthie scampered into the dark kitchen. Her bare feet were cold on the smooth floor. She dipped herself a glass of water and drank it, slowly. She shut her eyes.

Then she opened them. She put the glass in the sink and silently opened the pantry door. She took down the pickle jar with its quarter, pennies, nickels, and dimes. She went back to the living room. She had to hurry, because she knew that if she hesitated, she wouldn't do it.

"Here," she said, holding the jar out to her mother.

Mother anchored her needle in the collar of Joe's shirt and put the shirt back on the table. She took the jar from Ruthie. "What is this?" she asked.

Ruthie took a deep breath. She would not cry. "Joe needs things," she said. "He has only one suit and he has boots instead of shoes, and his hat doesn't look like the hats people wear in cities. I'm making him a handkerchief, but I can't make him a hat."

Mother put the jar on the table next to Joe's work pants. "You're right, Ruthie, we can't make him a hat, and he does need one," she said. "But you don't have to worry about it. Your father and

I can afford Joe's ticket to Philadelphia, and maybe even a new pair of shoes. Joe will be earning a salary soon. He can buy himself his own hat then."

"But he won't feel right in the beginning," Ruthie said. "He'll feel like a farmer. Folks might laugh at him if he doesn't have a city hat."

"No one will laugh at Joe," Mother said.

"They will, you know they will," Ruthie countered.

Mother looked grave. "You don't have to do this."

"I want to," Ruthie said. She tried to make her voice steady. "We could save up again—it wouldn't be so very much longer. Anyway, Joe is a lot more important than Clarinda."

"I'm glad you think so. Your brothers love you, Ruthie."

"I know," Ruthie said in a small voice.

"I do, too. I want you to know that. I love you."

"I know," Ruthie whispered. "Mother, I'm sorry. I'm trying to be a lady. I'll still try without Clarinda. I just thought she would be a help."

Mother bent and took Ruthie into her arms. "You *are* a lady," she said. "What you are doing is exactly what a lady would do.

"I am very proud of you," Mother continued. "You are a strong person and a good one. If I am to have only one daughter, I am grateful it is you."

Ruthie leaned hard against her mother's shoulder. She felt like she'd been waiting all her life to hear those words.

The next morning Mother hitched up the mare and she and Ruthie went into Fort Wayne to buy Joe a city hat at the finest store there. Ruthie tried not to flinch when all the Clarinda money disappeared.

On Easter Sunday the whole family drove to church in the surrey. Joe wore his new hat, and the new necktie that Hallie, Mallie, and Ruthie had made. He carried his new handkerchief. He was saving Mrs. Graber's stockings for the train. Ruthie thought he looked full-grown.

She sat beside him in her dress from last year. Paul sat on her other side. Across the aisle, Hallie and Mallie waved from their pew. Ruthie waved back. Bert squirmed in Mother's arms, and Ruthie reached across Paul and took him. She held him against her shoulder. He burped so loudly that people laughed two pews away.

The organist started the processional. The congregation stood. Ruthie remembered the words of the Christmas angel. "Fear not," she whispered to Joe, and he squeezed her hand and smiled. She still did not feel like a lady. But she felt important enough on her own.

25

The Errand in Town

❦

Summer came. With Joe gone, there was more work to do than ever. Ruthie missed him intensely. He almost never wrote, and when he did the letters were short and unsatisfying. He did not say anything about the factory. But he wrote that his hat was as fine as any in Philadelphia.

Mother began saving for Clarinda again, but Ruthie rarely counted the coins in the pickle jar. Her own sixteen cents were gone, and until harvest time came, Mother could not put aside more than a nickel a week. Clarinda might still be two years away. "I don't need that doll anymore," she told Mother. "I'll just play with Bert." She took Bert out for a stroll every afternoon; Hallie and Mallie took Sarah out too, and they walked together. No matter how busy they were, they always had time to do that.

"You never needed the doll," Mother said. "That doesn't mean you shouldn't get it."

Ruthie didn't try to explain what she meant. Clarinda was supposed to help her be a lady. It wasn't that she didn't want to be a lady anymore, and it wasn't that she already was one. She just didn't think the doll would help.

But she still wanted her—Clarinda was so fine and beautiful. Clarinda ought to have someone like Ruthie to love her. Sometimes in the twilight evenings Ruthie still sewed clothes for Clarinda. Other times she played tag in the orchard with the boys. The teams came out even now that Joe was gone.

In June Ruthie picked strawberries until she thought her back would break. In July they harvested the peaches. In August, while they waited for the rest of the crops to come in, Ruthie helped Mother can the garden vegetables. The kitchen was steamy and broiling hot. Ruthie hated it but did not complain.

At noon one day, Father came in smiling and spoke a few whispered words to Mother before he sat down. After dinner, Mother spoke up. "Ruthie, don't bother to clear. I need you to run an errand in town."

"I'll go," Paul volunteered quickly.

"Ruthie may," Mother said, to Ruthie's astonishment. She had never been asked to run an errand before.

"I'll put my shoes on," she said quickly. "May Hallie and Mallie come?"

Mother assented and so did Mrs. Graber. Hallie and Mallie washed their feet and put on their shoes. It would not do to be barefoot in town. Soon the three girls were walking down the road, arms linked.

"What do you have to do?" Mallie asked. They never ran errands, either.

"I'm to call at the post office for a package," Ruthie said.

"That's silly," Hallie said. "Your father was just there."

Ruthie shrugged. "Maybe the package wasn't ready." She didn't care. She was out of the kitchen, she was with Hallie and Mallie, and she was being trusted with an errand. She felt perfectly happy.

"Oh, no," Hallie groaned as they walked past the school. "Our first errand, and look who's there. Maude."

"Let's pretend we don't see her," Ruthie suggested. They swept haughtily past Maude into the post office. Maude looked disdainfully in the opposite direction. Mallie giggled.

The clerk at the post office smiled when he saw them. He lifted a big box off the back shelf and handed it across the counter to Ruthie. "It's yours, miss," he said.

Ruthie was amazed. The package was large but not heavy. Her very own name was written on the label: Ruth Hawk. "What is it?" she asked the clerk.

"I'm sure I don't know. Look at the return

mark, though. Came from Sears Roebuck. You been ordering something?"

"No." Ruthie took the box out to the front step and sat down. Hallie and Mallie hovered over her. Maude still stood by the road pretending not to see them.

"Open it," Hallie said.

"Maybe I should wait," Ruthie said. But her fingers were already ripping the paper. Inside the box was a great quantity of newspaper padding. On top of this lay a folded card. Ruthie opened it. The hand was unfamiliar, but the words were clear: " 'To Ruthie, with love from Joe,' " she read. "It's from Joe!" They hadn't heard from him in weeks.

Hallie giggled. "Maybe it's a hat."

"Open it!" Mallie urged.

But Ruthie knew in her heart what it was. She gently lifted the newspaper aside, then pulled apart a layer of tissue paper. The doll lay sleeping inside. Her long eyelashes rested on her fine bisque face and her hair curled in soft ringlets around her neck. She wore a dainty straw hat and

a coat of finest cashmere, and Ruthie knew that if she looked, she would find lace trimming on the doll's underwear.

Ruthie lifted the doll out of her nest and cradled her against her chest. The doll's eyelids swung open. "Hello, Clarinda," Ruthie said.

Author's Note

*R*uthie's Gift did not really happen, but it is still a true story.

My grandmother's name, until she was married, was Ruth Ann Hawk. She was the middle child of seven, the only girl, and she grew up on a small farm outside Cedarville, Indiana. When I was very small, she used to tell me stories about the times they had on the farm. She told me about playing Fox and Geese and Capture the Flag; about Paul's finger being chopped off by a gravestone; about the train that brought a doctor through a snowstorm to save her life.

Later, when I started writing, she told me more: about the little girls she played with, who dressed their cats like baby dolls; about the other little girls who refused to play with her at recess because she "wasn't a lady"; and about her two oldest brothers, who were sent to a Philadelphia factory during the war.

I changed a lot of specifics when I made her memories into a story. I bunched things that actually happened in different years all into the same year. I modeled Maude after a girl I knew and particularly detested. I made up a lot of things about the characters, including everything they thought and said. Ruthie my grandmother and Ruthie my character are not the same, but I think they would have understood each other well.

My grandmother worked in a factory after high school until she saved enough money to go to college. She earned a degree from what is now Ball State University and taught until the Depression closed her school. She married my grandfather, Charles Brubaker, when she was thirty-three years old; she had my father two years later and my aunt seven years after that.

I knew all Ruthie's brothers except Joe, who

died before I was born. I loved Paul best. When my grandfather died, I was four and my brother was two weeks old. Paul stepped in to fill our grandfather's place at birthdays and holiday dinners. Paul was an adventurer. After he had retired from his job as a train conductor, he often spent summers panning for gold in Alaska. He gave my brother arrowheads and came to my ballet recitals. He died quietly when I was sixteen, and I still miss him.

Grandma turned ninety years old a few months after *Ruthie's Gift* was accepted for publication. She helped me with details and research, read my first draft, and was as happy as I was to watch it turn into this book. "I think they all would have liked it," she told me. "Especially Joe—I think he would have been proud."

Read more about Ruthie and her friends
in *One-of-a-Kind Mallie*.

Turn the page for a preview of the novel.

0-385-32694-7

Delacorte Press

Excerpt from *One-of-a-Kind Mallie*
by Kimberly Brubaker Bradley
Copyright © 1999 by Kimberly Brubaker Bradley

Published by Delacorte Press
a division of Random House, Inc.
1540 Broadway, New York, New York 10036

All rights reserved

1

Identical?

Mallie Graber sat in the schoolyard under the shade of a sycamore tree. She had picked a pile of dandelion flowers and was braiding them into a crown. The sun blazed. Mallie's flowers hung limp in her hands. Across the yard, the air above the school's war garden seemed to shimmer. The potato plants and cabbages lay covered in brown dust. Mallie knew they were not dying. She had helped water them only that morning. But they looked like they were dying.

Mallie felt like a wilted cabbage. Her stockings and shoes were smothering her, and so was her wool school dress. She wished someone would pour a bucket of water over her head.

In three days school would be over. Mallie couldn't wait.

"Mallie! Hey, Mallie! Come play with us!"

Mallie looked up. Her sister, Hallie, and their friend Ruthie waved. Ruthie held up a jump rope.

"It's too hot," Mallie said.

"Mallie!" Hallie marched across the yard, Ruthie right behind. "We need a third person. Come on."

Mallie leaned against the trunk of the tree. "It's too hot," she said. She tied the ends of her crown together and twirled it in her hands.

Hallie sighed. "It's not hot. There are only ten minutes of recess left. We finally got the jump rope away from Alice."

Mallie didn't move. Hallie nudged her with a foot. "It's not hot."

"It is for me," Mallie said. "Get someone else." She put the crown of flowers on her head.

"But we want you," Ruthie said.

"Sit down," Mallie offered. "There's plenty of room in the shade."

Ruthie sat. "I'm so hot I could die."

Mallie patted her crown into place. Like Ruthie and Hallie, she wore her hair in two long braids, with ribbons tied in bows on the ends. Mallie had three sets of hair ribbons. Some of the other girls had six or even seven sets. Ruthie had four. Sometimes Hallie or Mallie switched with her on the way to school so it looked like they all had more.

Hallie never switched with Mallie, of course, because their ribbons were exactly alike. Their stockings, shoes, skirts, blouses, and dresses were all exactly alike. Even their underwear was the same.

Their faces were exactly the same. Their smiles, side by side, looked exactly alike. Their eyes were the same color and their ears the same shape. Mallie and Hallie were identical twins—the only twins in Cedarville, the only twins they knew. Except for the front tooth Hallie had chipped two years earlier falling off a seesaw, there was no way, looking at them, to tell them apart.

Hallie snorted. "You look silly in that crown," she said. "Flower chains are for babies. You're ten years old. Fourth-graders who are almost fifth-graders don't play with dandelions."

"Piffle," Mallie said. "This one does." She jammed another flower into the front of her crown so that it hung over her forehead like the forelock of a horse. She bobbed her head. The flower danced. "That's better."

Hallie snatched the flower out and flung it away. "Jump rope with us!" she said.

"Don't be rude," Ruthie told Hallie. She got to her feet. "Please. We need three people," she said to Mallie.

Mallie heaved a great sigh and stood up. "First you have to apologize," she told Hallie.

"I'm sorry," Hallie said.

"And give me my flower back."

Hallie rolled her eyes, but she plucked the dandelion out of the dirt and stuffed it into Mallie's crown. Mallie shook her head to make sure it felt right. "Okay," she said. "I'll play."

"I just hope nobody thinks I'm you," Hallie said. She handed Mallie one end of the rope.

"Keep your mouth open, then."

To Mallie's disgust, Hallie did. She jumped rope with her teeth bared like a tiger's so that everyone could see her broken tooth.

Mallie didn't think that tooth was something Hallie should display. Still, she guessed she understood. When her turn came to jump, she held on to her crown with one hand. However much Hallie wanted to be different from her, it was only a tenth as much as she wanted to be different from Hallie. Mallie would have given a thousand dollars in gold not to be a twin.

2

One Poem for Two

The bell rang. The pupils trailed inside. Miss Lane, the schoolteacher, sat at her desk and wiped her forehead with her handkerchief. Inside was hotter than outside. Every window was open, but there was no breeze. Mallie felt sweat trickle along her scalp beneath her crown.

"Hallie." Miss Lane spoke softly. Mallie looked up. Miss Lane nodded at Mallie's head.

"I'm Mallie," Mallie whispered.

"Mallie," Miss Lane corrected herself. "Put the flowers away, please."

Mallie got up and dumped them into her lunch pail. Miss Lane always confused her with

Hallie. Mr. Ames, their old teacher, never had. He was in the navy now.

"Thank you," Miss Lane said. She began to call pupils forward. They all had poems to memorize for the school picnic on Saturday.

Hallie squirmed in her seat. "I told you," she said.

Mallie gave her an evil look. "It wasn't because the flowers were babyish."

"But they were," Hallie said. Mallie stuck out her tongue.

"Hallie and Mallie." For a moment Mallie thought they were in trouble, but it was just their turn to recite. She followed Hallie to the front of the classroom.

Miss Lane smiled. "Let's hear how you two are coming along," she said.

Suddenly Mallie's blood boiled over. "Why 'you two'?" she said. "Why not 'you' and 'you,' separate? Why didn't we get our own poems?"

Miss Lane had assigned them a single long poem, "The Wreck of the *Hesperus*," to say together. It was a thrilling piece about a shipwreck. Until that moment, Mallie had loved it.

"Everyone else got their own poem," Mallie

went on. "I don't want to recite with Hallie. I want my own poem." She looked at Hallie. "Don't you?"

"No," Hallie said. "I like saying it with you."

"Well, I don't." Mallie realized the other students were staring. She dropped her voice. "May I have my own poem, please?"

Miss Lane shook her head. "You should have asked three weeks ago. The picnic is on Saturday, Mallie. You can't learn a new poem in three days."

"Yes, I can." Mallie stubbed her foot against a raised plank in the floor.

"*I* can't!" Hallie crossed her arms. "I don't want to, either."

Miss Lane nodded. "I'm sorry, Mallie. I wish you'd told me your feelings before. Next year you may have your own poem. Let me hear 'The Wreck of the *Hesperus*' now."

Mallie felt her chin quiver. "Mr. Ames would have given me my own poem," she said.

She heard Hallie hiss in disbelief. She heard one of the older pupils laugh.

Miss Lane frowned, but she didn't look angry. She never did. Miss Lane didn't care how they felt about her; she didn't love teaching the way Mr. Ames had. She did it because it was her duty in this time of war.

"You'll have to write me an essay," she said. "One hundred words, due tomorrow, on the subject of impertinence."

"Yes, ma'am," Mallie said, looking at the floor. Hallie took a step closer. Mallie stepped away.

When school let out, all the girls walked down the street together. Cedarville was too small to have its own Red Cross chapter, but it had a knitting circle that met every Wednesday afternoon for two hours. All the women in town, and all the girls down to the first-graders, belonged. They knit things for the brave soldiers fighting overseas. So far Mallie alone had made thirteen washcloths, twenty pairs of stockings, a sweater, and three mufflers; Hallie had matched her. It was all plain knitting of the most boring sort. It was their duty to do it.

The grown women went to Red Cross meetings in Leo and Fort Wayne as well. They made bandages and raised money for war relief.

In the evenings, Miss Lane taught nursing classes at the Red Cross.

"Mallie Graber," said Maude, an older girl Mallie detested, "I never heard anyone sass a teacher like you." She swished her skirt in front of Mallie. "Your mother will be ashamed."

Mallie bit her lip.

"Won't she?" Maude persisted.

Mallie still didn't say anything.

"Are *you* going to tell her, Maude?" Ruthie asked. "I should have known you'd snitch."

Maude tossed her head. "I just feel sorry for *Hallie*. To have a sister like that."

Mallie looked at Hallie. To her surprise, Hallie looked away. She hunched her shoulders and walked faster.

Mallie turned to Ruthie. "What's wrong with Hallie?"

Ruthie looked uncomfortable. "You told the whole school you didn't want to say a poem with her."

"I didn't mean it that way. I just wanted my own poem."

Ruthie shrugged. "Same thing."

"No, it isn't." Mallie swung her knitting bag in frustration.

Ruthie pointed across the street. "There're our mothers," she said. Mrs. Hawk and Mrs. Graber were pushing their baby carriages out of McClennan's general store. Mallie's little sister, Sarah, and Ruthie's littlest brother, Bert, were both almost two years old.

"Mallie!" Sarah saw Mallie and waved. Mallie ran across the street and buried her face in Sarah's hair. She breathed in Sarah's sweet smell.

Mallie's mother kissed her. "How was school?"

Mallie piled her knitting bag and books into the carriage beside Sarah and pushed it along the sidewalk. "Not too good," she said at last.

"I know it's hard to sit still and learn in this heat," Mrs. Graber said. "Perhaps Mrs. Ellis will have lemonade for us."

Mrs. Ellis, a widow with no children, was hosting the knitting circle that day. She made Mallie itch. Going to her house was not worth an entire pitcher of lemonade.

Mother squeezed Mallie's shoulder. "I expect you to be polite," she said. "Where's Hallie?"

Mallie waved her hand. "Up there. She's in a horrible mood."

Mother looked concerned. "That's not like her."

"It's not my fault," Mallie said. "I didn't do anything wrong."